free REIN

Fight to the Finish

free REIN

Fight to the Finish

by

Catherine Hapka

Based on the original TV series created by
Vicki Lutas and Anna McCleery

Scholastic Inc.

All rights reserved. Published by Scholastic Inc., *Publishers since 1920*.
SCHOLASTIC and associated logos are trademarks and/or
registered trademarks of Scholastic Inc.

ISBN 978-1-338-30449-7

10 9 8 7 6 5 4 3 2   18 19 20 21 22
Printed in U.S.A.   40

First printing 2018

Book design by Jessica Meltzer

To everyone
who cherishes friendship
and riding together

1
Breaking News

"Easy, Raven. What is it, boy?" Zoe Phillips stepped back as the big black horse she was grooming suddenly lifted his head and pawed at the floor. He was tied in his stall, so he couldn't go far. But he pricked his ears toward the door and snorted.

Zoe smiled, admiring how beautiful her horse was. Sometimes she still felt like pinching herself when she looked at Raven—especially when she remembered he belonged to her now. But this was a dream she never wanted to wake up from!

"Zoe!" Suddenly, Becky burst into the stall, breathless and pink cheeked. "There you are!"

"Where else would she be, silly?" Jade stepped into view behind Becky, smiling and shaking her head. "Sorry, Raven, we didn't mean to spook you."

"He's all right." Zoe gave Raven a pat, then stepped toward her friends. Together, the three of them made up the Pony Squad. "I was about to tack him up for a ride. What's going on?"

"Something utterly amazing is going to happen—right here at Bright Field Stables!" Becky exclaimed, her blond braids practically quivering with enthusiasm. "I'm serious, Zoe. This is big news! As in, big, big, big!"

"And just when things were getting back to normal around here . . ." Zoe traded a smile with Jade. The three of them had recently helped thwart a crooked race promoter who'd been up to no good. Now that it was autumn, the friends were excited about their upcoming fall break.

But that wasn't the only adventure that had befallen Zoe since moving from Los Angeles to this little island off the coast of England. Her mother had grown up here, and her grandfather still lived in an old brick house just beyond the stable grounds. Ever since she had met Raven, her world had turned upside down. He'd been almost totally wild then, and she'd been the only person who was able to calm him down. That was how she'd ended up at Bright Field Stables . . . and her life had changed forever.

"Okay," she said, smiling at Becky. "What's the big news?"

"Poppy Addison!" Becky cried. "She's coming! As in, here! As in, soon! As in, O, capital M, capital G!"

Before Zoe could ask who Poppy Addison was and why her arrival was so exciting, they were joined by Mia and Susie. Mia and Susie weren't Zoe's friends, exactly, but they both kept horses at Bright Fields, too. In fact, Mia had owned several horses when Zoe had first met her—including Raven. And her wealthy father, Elliott MacDonald, used to own Bright Fields.

But recently the Bright Fields stable hand, Pin Hawthorne, had discovered that he was actually a duke—and worth more money than anyone else on the island! He'd bought the stables from Mr. MacDonald and rebuilt it after a fire had destroyed much of the place. Now Pin was off traveling the world to places he never thought he'd have the money to see.

Where are you right now, Pin? Zoe wondered, her heart thumping at the thought of him. She'd felt a connection with Pin from the start, even back in his stable hand days when he'd been prickly and suspicious. In some ways, things were even more complicated now that he was a duke. It was hard not having him around in person—especially since Zoe still wasn't sure exactly where they stood, relationship-wise. She couldn't wait to see him whenever he finally returned to the island for good.

In the meantime, Mia was acting a bit more humble these days—or, at least, she seemed to be trying to. Pin had bought Raven for Zoe, and Mia was back to focusing on her favorite horse, a lovely and talented gray gelding named Firefly. The two of them had been winning at shows together for years, and they had a bond almost as special as the one Zoe had with Raven.

"Did you tell Zoe about the clinic yet?" Susie asked, her blue eyes sparkling with excitement. "It's happening this fall break!"

"I don't know why you're all so eager to tell Zoe about it." Mia wrinkled her nose as she glanced at Raven. "I mean, Raven isn't exactly a dressage horse, is he? Besides, clinics aren't meant for beginner riders."

"Huh?" Zoe looked from one girl to the next, more confused than ever. "What's a clinic? And who's this Poppy person?"

Becky's eyes widened even more. "Don't tell me you've never heard of Poppy Addison!"

Jade poked her on the shoulder. "Of course she hasn't. Zoe's still fairly new to this horse stuff, remember? Plus, she's American—Poppy probably isn't as famous over in the States."

Zoe smiled. That was pure Jade—sensible, rational, always looking for answers. She was as levelheaded and logical as Becky was happy-go-lucky and creative. And Zoe loved them both exactly the way they were.

"Well, on this island, Poppy's a total rock star," Susie declared. "Right, Mia?"

"Absolutely. That's why my father invited her to do a clinic here when he heard she and her teammates had an opening in their schedule." Mia shrugged. "Naturally, he made sure I was the first rider signed up to ride."

Zoe shook her head. "Whoa, slow down, people. Still not fully up to speed on what's going on here."

"Sorry." Jade smiled. "Poppy Addison is a famous dressage rider. She grew up right here on the island—"

"With my dad," Mia broke in. "They're great friends. More like family, really—he calls her the little sister he never had."

Becky nodded. "And now she's on the national equestrian team! Like, the one going to the next Olympics! Isn't that cool?"

"Totally cool," Zoe agreed. "So is a clinic like a riding demonstration or something?"

"Almost. A clinic is more like an extended lesson," Jade explained.

"Yeah, but only if you think Oxford University is like an extended primary school!" Becky exclaimed. "It's definitely higher riding education. Ride-u-cation? Higher-rider-cation?"

"No, Jade is exactly right." Susie jumped in. "A clinic really is like a super-intensive lesson with the best instructors around. Poppy has been traveling all over the UK with two of her fellow riders from the national dressage team. They stop at different stables, and the three of them teach a group of riders over the course of a full day at each place. It's a way for everyone to improve their skills by riding with the best, you know?"

"Oh! Cool." Zoe glanced at Raven, who was nosing at his hay net. "So can anyone sign up to ride?"

"No!" Mia said quickly. "I mean, there are a limited number of spots. So you might already be too late. Besides, it's quite expensive—much more than a regular lesson."

"Well, I've already signed up," Susie said with a happy sigh. "I can't believe the luck of Poppy coming here now of all times! Darcy and I have been focusing on our dressage ever since Junior Nationals, and Marcus says we're coming along well."

Zoe nodded. Darcy was Susie's horse, an elegant bay mare. The two of them were primarily jumpers, but Darcy was what Bright Fields's head trainer, Marcus, called an all-rounder—a horse that could do just about anything.

"Okay, all I know about dressage is that it doesn't involve jumping, which means I haven't paid that much attention to it so far," Zoe said with a laugh. "It's basically just fancy flatwork set to music, right? Like the hip-hop routine Becky and Bob did at the County Show?" Bob was the shaggy Irish Cob that Becky shared with her younger brother.

"There's not always music involved," Jade said. "What Becky and Bob did was called a musical freestyle."

Susie nodded. "Only a few dressage shows do that."

"Right. That's why Bob and I don't compete much," Becky added. "If there's no hip-hop involved, he tends to get bored and start inventing his own movements."

"So non-Bob dressage is fancy flatwork *without* music, then." Zoe smiled and gave Raven a rub on the neck. "Raven and I can probably handle that."

"Don't be so sure, Zoe," Mia said. "There's a lot more to dressage than just walk, trot, canter. You have to perform a test—"

"That's sort of like following a course in jumping," Susie put in helpfully. "A dressage test lays out a pattern of moves you have to ride in a certain order."

"What kinds of moves?" Zoe asked.

Mia sighed. "If you have to ask . . ."

"Bob and I can show you some moves, Zoe," Becky offered.

Mia snorted. "Yeah, right. I'm *so* sure that *Bob* is the one who'll catch a future Olympian's eye."

"Thanks, Becky. That would be great." Zoe traded an amused look with Jade. Bob wasn't exactly fancy—but he definitely had a lot of personality!

"By the way, you haven't even heard the best part yet," Mia added, tossing her long brown hair over one shoulder. "Poppy will be staying at my house while she's back on the island. She's even arriving a couple of days earlier than her teammates so she and my dad can catch up." She shot a smug smile around the group. "Like I said, she's practically family. It'll be such fun getting to know her better."

"Oh, lucky!" Susie cried. "Do you suppose she'll spend much time here at the yard? It would be awesome having her around for the extra couple of days!"

Becky let out a squeak. "Not just awesome—*horse-some*! I mean, a real equestrian celebrity, right here at our little stables? Wow!"

Mia frowned. "Well, I suppose Poppy will probably want to see the yard. But I'm sure she'll be a bit busy, so you probably shouldn't pester her too much."

"We'll try to contain ourselves," Jade said, rolling her eyes.

"When does Poppy arrive?" Susie asked Mia eagerly. "I can't wait to get her input on Darcy. I'm sure she'll have lots of amazing tips to help us progress."

"Tomorrow afternoon." Mia shrugged. "But like I said, I expect she'll be pretty busy. You might not see much of her before the clinic, unless she decides to stop by and meet Firefly or something."

Zoe was a little surprised. Normally, Mia seemed to enjoy having Susie around to fawn over everything she did. But this time she seemed eager to have Poppy Addison all to herself.

Well, Mia was never great at sharing, Zoe reminded herself. *But she'll have to share Poppy with Susie during the clinic—and maybe with me and Raven, too. Because it sounds like exactly the kind of new challenge we need right now!*

2

Trying New Things

"We'll be focusing on dressage from now until the clinic, for those who are thinking of riding with Poppy." Marcus smiled at the half dozen young riders gathered around him in Bright Fields's riding ring later that day. "That way you'll be up to speed for the clinic. Now that your horses are warmed up, let's start with something simple—leg yields." As usual he looked dapper in his breeches and boots, more than living up to the nickname Becky and Jade had given him: "Hot Marcus."

"Only dressage lessons for a while, huh?" Zoe murmured to Raven, gathering up her reins. She glanced over at the brightly colored jumps, which someone had left in a pile outside the gate. "Okay, Raven. We both caught on to jumping pretty fast. Let's see if we can figure out this dressage stuff, too, huh? I think we're up for it."

She sent him walking along the rail after Jade, who was riding her favorite horse, a handsome ex–police mount named Major.

"All right, working walk, everyone," Marcus called out, clapping his hands to set the pace. "One, two, one, two . . . Now leg yield your horses away from the rail, please."

Zoe blinked. "Um, say what now?" she called out.

In front of her, she saw that Major had started moving sideways while he was also still walking forward. After a few strides, he was a yard or so in from the rail.

"Oh, never mind," Zoe said. "Leg yield is a fancy dressage way of saying go sideways, right? Got it."

She nudged at Raven's right side with her leg. At the same time, she gave a gentle pull on his left rein. Raven tossed his head and spun to the inside, snorting.

"Halt, everyone," Marcus called out. "Hang on, Zoe. Let's talk through this."

"Sure." Feeling a bit sheepish, Zoe brought Raven to a stop.

"Can't you give her a remedial lesson later?" Mia called. "Some of us want to move on to the real stuff."

"Everyone can do with a refresher on the basics, Mia," Marcus chided with a smile. "And a leg yield is one of the most basic dressage moves there is."

"Well, that explains it," Zoe said with a laugh. "Raven and I are brand-new to this dressage stuff. We're jumpers, remember?"

"Yes, well, leg yielding is a very useful skill for a jumping horse as well," Marcus told her. "Suppose you're coming in a bit crooked to a big jump—wouldn't it be useful to be able to signal for your horse to take a couple of steps over before he gets there? That's leg yielding. Basically."

"Oh! I get it. Cool." Zoe smiled. Sometimes it felt as if there was so much to learn about riding that she'd never be able to learn it all. But it was fun to try!

"Now, you already know that horses are trained to move away from pressure, yes?" Marcus said. "For instance, if I give Darcy a poke in her left shoulder"—he stepped over to Susie's horse and demonstrated—"she'll move away from my hand toward the right. See?"

Susie smiled as Darcy obediently took a step away from Marcus. "She's brilliant about that," she said. "I barely have to think of nudging her and she responds."

"You hear that, Raven?" Zoe patted her horse. "You can't let Darcy show you up—let's try this again!"

Marcus chuckled. "Okay, go for it, Zoe. Right leg on—no, don't use your reins too much or he'll think you want him to turn . . ."

"Oops!" Zoe blushed as Raven spun in again, nearly bumping into Marcus. "Sorry, guess I'm the one who messed up that time."

"Try it again." Marcus sounded as patient as ever.

"You can do it, Zoe and Raven!" Becky cheered, dropping Bob's reins to give Zoe a double thumbs-up. Bob took the opportunity to step sideways—a perfect leg yield, Zoe figured—and stretched his neck under the fence to grab a mouthful of grass.

Jade and Susie added their own words of encouragement. But Mia rolled her eyes and sighed loudly. "I'll be working on some more *advanced* moves over here, if you don't mind," she said loudly before riding Firefly off toward the far end of the ring.

Marcus ignored her departure. "All right, Zoe, let's give it one more go," he said. "This time, instead of signaling with one rein, you'll want to move them both slightly to the inside, which in this case is your left—like this." He reached up and grabbed Zoe's hands, showing her how to move the reins.

"Okay, everyone try it one more time—go!" Marcus called out.

Zoe set Raven walking after Major again. This time, she nudged with her right leg first, then very carefully moved both hands to the inside as Marcus had showed her. At first nothing happened except that Raven sped up a little.

But when she repeated her aids, it happened—he took a step to the side!

"Hey!" she cried. "We're doing it! Aren't we? I think we're doing it!"

Marcus laughed. "You're doing it," he agreed. "Keep going!"

Zoe asked for a leg yield again. This time Raven shook his head and went a little crooked, but he still moved over as she'd asked.

"Wow, this dressage stuff is kind of fun, isn't it, boy?" Zoe said to Raven, patting him with a smile.

An hour later, however, she wasn't so sure she was having that much fun anymore. She and Raven were pretty good at leg yielding once they got the hang of it. The other dressage moves? Not so much. There was the "shoulder-in," which Zoe still didn't quite understand. The "turn on the forehand" was even worse. She was supposed to get Raven to plant his front hooves and rotate the rest of his body around. But every time they tried it, he ended up prancing in place, backing up, or tossing his head.

"Never mind, Zoe," Marcus said after their fourth or fifth try. "He's just getting confused now. We'll work on it more another time."

Zoe wanted to argue. She hated giving up before she conquered something! Every other horse in the ring could do a turn on the forehand—so she was sure they could, too, if they just tried a little harder. But then Raven snorted and pawed, and she realized Marcus was right. This wasn't just about her. She'd pushed Raven too hard before and learned her lesson.

"Okay, boy." She loosened the reins and gave her horse a pat. "I think we did okay for our first time doing dressage, anyway."

"Too right." Marcus smiled and winked, then turned to check on the rest of the class.

Zoe slumped in her saddle and sighed, watching Mia and Firefly execute a perfect turn on the forehand. "We'll get there, Raven," she whispered. A few minutes later, the Pony Squad had tied their horses at the hitching rail in the yard so they could talk while they unsaddled and groomed them. "That was a fun lesson, wasn't it?" Jade commented.

"Uh-huh. Bob loved it." Becky peered at the others over her pony's broad back. "Raven did pretty well for his first time. You too, Zoe."

"Yeah, right." Zoe rolled her eyes. "I'm starting to think Mia's right—Raven and I need the remedial class."

Her friends traded a look. "Or maybe not," Jade said. "I mean, when I had trouble catching on to trigonometry last year, my mum and dad didn't send me back to primary school to review basic arithmetic. They hired the best PhD mathematician on the island to tutor me until I got the hang of it."

"Really? That's amazing!" Zoe exclaimed.

"Uh-huh." Jade nodded. "They interviewed four people before they settled on one."

"No, not that part—I totally believe your parents would do that." Zoe grinned. "What I can't believe is that you actually had trouble with math once upon a time!"

Becky snorted with laughter. "Good one, Zoe!"

Jade smiled. "*So* not the point," she said. "What I'm saying is that maybe this clinic is the perfect chance for you and Raven to have a crash course in dressage." She shrugged and turned away to set Major's saddle and girth on the rail nearby. "I mean, you've come a long way in a short time, but there's still tons to learn. Why not learn it from the best of the best if you've got the chance?"

Zoe smiled, glad that her friends were in tune with her thinking, as always. "You're absolutely right, Jade."

She gave her horse a pat. "That clinic is *exactly* what Raven and I need right now!" Now all Zoe had to do was see if her mom agreed . . .

A couple of hours later, Zoe opened the front door of her grandfather's house to a whirlwind of pink glitter rushing down the stairs.

"Coming through!" Rosie cried.

Zoe jumped back just in time to avoid being thwacked with the stack of dusty framed pictures her little sister was carrying. "Hello to you, too," she said with a laugh.

She followed Rosie into the comfortably cluttered kitchen, where her mother and grandfather were sitting at the table drinking tea. "Mom! Gramps!" Rosie exclaimed. "Check out what I found in the attic." She dropped the pictures on the table, spreading them out for a better view. "Amazing, right?"

"*You* were in the attic?" Zoe said. "I thought you claimed to be allergic to dust. Or was that allergic to old junk that should have been thrown away forty years ago?"

"Junk?" Their grandfather put a hand to his heart, feigning offense. "I'll have you know those are my treasures!" He leaned over for a better look at the framed paintings. "Mmm, especially these . . . ," he added in a quieter voice.

Zoe took a better look, too. One of the paintings showed a landscape full of pink roses. Another was a busy, active, familiar scene at the local town pier. Others featured different places, people, and animals.

"Oh, I like this one!" Zoe picked up a painting of a girl riding a pretty gray pony. She peered at the wild black curls escaping from beneath the rider's hard hat. "Wait—Mom, is this you?"

"Oh, I forgot all about that." Her mother tucked a strand of curly black hair behind one ear, then took the painting from Zoe. "Yes, Mum painted me and Emerald as a surprise for my eleventh birthday."

Zoe was impressed. The horse in the painting looked so alive that she wanted to reach out and feed it an apple.

Meanwhile, Rosie's eyes widened. "I was right!" she cried. "I thought that signature looked familiar . . . so Grandma painted all these?" She swept a pink-manicured hand over the pile of pictures.

"Yes, she was very talented." Grampa picked up a painting of a gnarled old tree on a bluff overlooking the sea. He gestured at Zoe's mom with a smile. "That's where Maggie got her love of art."

"I guess it runs in the family," Rosie said. "Because I could tell these paintings were of truly superb quality as soon as I saw them."

"Could you now?" her mother said, trading an amused glance with Grampa.

"Of course!" Rosie picked up a painting of a bird and studied it. "This one, for instance—the color, the light, the movement. It's inspiring! You should really have these hanging up around the house, Gramps. They would definitely impress your visitors."

"I suppose they would," he agreed with a chuckle. "Let's do it."

"Great." Rosie smiled. "But don't take up all the wall space, okay? Because I decided I'm going to start painting, too."

"You are?" Her mother raised an eyebrow. "Hmm, you weren't interested when I offered to get you art lessons back in LA."

"In case you haven't noticed, we're not in LA anymore." Rosie shrugged. "This is the home of our ancestral family talent. It's, like, super inspiring. I've realized I want to paint. I *need* to paint."

"Great, so paint, then," Zoe put in, eager to change the subject to the clinic. "Now, if that's settled . . ."

Rosie ignored her. "Everyone is always saying that Zoe's true talent is riding," she said. "Maybe my true talent is art! I mean, I've always had an amazing eye for fashion and color and stuff like that, so it totally makes sense." She glanced at her mother. "Mom, can we go to the mainland? I want to get some art supplies."

Her mother looked alarmed. "Hold on a second. I'm all for you trying painting, Rosie. But we're not buying a lot of expensive supplies until you decide whether you like it. You can use your gran's old paints for now."

Grampa nodded. "I'll help you find them if you like," he told Rosie. "I think they're still around here somewhere."

Zoe's mom chuckled. "Everything you have ever owned is still 'around here somewhere,' Dad," she said fondly.

"And see how that comes in handy?" He winked at Zoe.

She smiled back. "Speaking of big news," she began, "I was just at the stables, and—"

"Oh, the stables!" Rosie exclaimed. "I almost forgot to tell you, I need to buy a new bridle for Prince."

"What?" her mother exclaimed.

"Why do you need to buy him a bridle?" Zoe added. "He already has one. And he's not actually your horse, you know."

She was still surprised that her little sister had decided to start riding. When they'd all arrived on the island, Rosie had worn a perpetual look of disgust whenever she went anywhere near the stables. She'd complained non-stop about the big, hairy beasts with their seemingly endless supply of poop.

But eventually, the horses had won her over. She was taking lessons on a sweet pony named Prince, though Zoe suspected her sister spent more time braiding his mane and painting his hooves glitter pink than she did riding him.

"I know." Rosie shrugged. "But he stepped on his reins and broke them right after my lesson yesterday, so I told Marcus I'd get him a new pair. I saw these amazing ones online—they've got pink and white crystals on them with a matching bridle, and—"

"Rosie!" her mother exclaimed. "First new paints, and now a new bridle. Do you think I'm made of money? You can buy Prince a new pair of reins—plain leather ones—with your own money."

"What?" Rosie squawked loudly.

Her mother crossed her arms over her chest. "If a horse steps on his reins, it's nearly always the rider's fault," she said. "Perhaps next time you'll remember not to be so careless, mmm? Horses are expensive, and it's best you learn that up front."

Zoe hid a smile at Rosie's outraged expression. But it faded quickly.

Mom's right, she thought. *Horses are expensive—and so is that clinic.*

Before leaving the stables earlier, she'd checked with Marcus about the price to ride with Poppy and her teammates—it was much higher than she'd expected. How could Zoe ask for that kind of money? Especially when her mother had always been so supportive and never complained about Raven's expenses so far?

Her mother's voice broke into her thoughts. "What were you going to say about the stables today, Zoe?" she asked.

Zoe quickly picked up one of her grandmother's paintings and studied it to avoid her mother's gaze. "Nothing," she said. "Just that I had fun, that's all."

Her heart was breaking at the thought of her and Raven missing their chance to learn from Olympic-level riders. But it looked like this new challenge would be a little *too* challenging to pull off after all.

No Money, More Problems

Ready to hit the stables?" Rosie sang out as she skipped downstairs the next morning.

Zoe glanced up from tying her paddock boots. Her eyes widened. "What are you wearing?"

"Do you like it? Now that I'm going to be a famous painter, I figured I should look the part." Rosie did a little spin. She was dressed in sparkly silver leggings, her favorite pink high-tops, and a long white smock dotted with rhinestones and multicolored paint splatters. Perched on her head was a hot-pink beret.

"Very artsy," Zoe agreed. "Might be hard to ride in that smock, though."

Rosie grabbed a pile of art supplies from the table. "Oh, I'm not planning to ride today. I'm going to do some sketches of Prince. I already have an idea for a fabulous painting of him. Maybe a whole series! Enough to fill a gallery, probably."

"Okay, whatever." Zoe tied off her boot and stood up. "Let's get moving, Rosie van Gogh."

When they reached the yard, Rosie wandered off in the direction of Prince's stall. Zoe glanced around and spotted Jade and Becky in the central courtyard. Bob was tied at the fence. Jade was picking burrs out of one side of his shaggy mane, while Becky struggled to work a comb through the other side. They both looked up when Zoe hurried toward them.

"Did you ask about the clinic?" Becky demanded eagerly. "My parents said I can use the birthday money I got from my aunt and uncle to help pay for it, though I'm going to have to work twenty-four hours a day at the café to cover the rest."

"Any chance I could pick up some shifts, too?" Zoe joked weakly. Becky worked at the popular Barley Bag Café after school and on weekends to help earn Bob's keep.

"What? Why?" Becky gasped and dropped her comb. "Oh no—don't tell me your mum said no as well?"

"As well?" Zoe glanced at Jade. "Does that mean you can't do the clinic, either?"

Jade shook her head. "I just spent all my money on a new microscope for my advanced science module," she said, flicking a burr off into the grass. "I tried to talk my parents into paying for the clinic as an early birthday gift, but they didn't go for it."

"Probably because your birthday's months away," Becky pointed out.

Jade sighed. "That's not it. If it were a university prep class or science fair entry or something, I'm sure they'd pay for it in a heartbeat. Paying that much for a riding clinic is another story."

"Whatever their reasons, this is terrible!" Becky exclaimed. "Zoe, why can't you do it? Don't tell me your mum's getting all weird about you riding again."

"No, nothing like that." Zoe quickly filled them in on the situation. "So unless I win the lottery in the next few days, I guess Raven and I won't be doing the clinic after all."

"Never mind." Jade gave her a hug. "We can watch Becky and the others ride in the clinic, yeah? We'll still be able to learn a lot that way."

"I guess." Zoe didn't think watching the clinic sounded nearly as exciting as riding in it. But she supposed she would have to settle for what she could get.

Becky looked dismayed. "But it won't be the same without you two!" she cried, draping her arms over Bob's neck and staring at her friends. "Maybe we can come up with a way to earn money. Oh! I know—a bake sale! I can make my famous carrot cupcakes—"

"And have Bob eat them all again, like he did at the last bake sale we tried to put on?" Jade smiled and patted the spotted pony. "In any case, there's no way we can sell enough cupcakes to pay for two clinic entries."

"Okay, no bake sale." Becky looked undaunted. "But I'm sure we can come up with a moneymaking scheme that'll work. I know! We could set up a fortune-telling booth at the pier. People love hearing the future, right? We could all wear long robes and mysterious hats." She frowned as Zoe and Jade shook their heads. "Okay, then maybe we could find a TV game show to enter. People win loads of money on those."

"Becky, the clinic is only a few days away!" Jade reminded her. "We don't have time to be on a game show before then."

"Maybe we could ask the bank for a loan," Becky said. "You know—against our future game show winnings."

Zoe laughed. "Or we could film you asking the bank for that kind of loan," she joked. "Their reaction would be so hilarious it'd be sure to go viral online."

"Yes!" Becky cried. "And then we could put it on my blog and charge advertisers to put ads on the video!"

Zoe and Jade were both laughing by now. "Thanks, Becky," Jade said. "We really appreciate your efforts. But I'm afraid it's just too late."

"Yeah." Zoe sighed. "I wish there was some way to enter that clinic. But Jade's right—it's too late to figure out a way to get that much money."

Mia and Susie hurried over just in time to hear what Zoe had said. "Oh, you can't afford the clinic, Zoe?" Mia said quickly. "Too bad. But never mind—as I said, it'd probably be too advanced for you and Raven anyhow. Right, Susie?"

"Oh, I don't know, I'm sure they'd be fine." Susie sounded distracted. "But never mind that—did you hear?" She smiled at Zoe and her friends.

"Hear what?" Zoe asked, reaching over to pull a twig out of Bob's mane.

Susie clapped her hands. "Poppy's arrived on the island! Mia's dad just went to pick her up at the ferry. And he said she insists on coming to the yard first thing!"

"She's coming *here*?" Becky let out a squeal and smacked her pony on the neck. "Did you hear that, Bob? You're about to meet Poppy Addison!"

At that moment, Rosie wandered toward them with a large sketch pad tucked under one arm and Prince trailing along behind her on a lead rope. "What's with all the noise out here?" she complained. "I'm trying to focus on my art!"

"I can see that." Zoe stared at Prince. Rosie had painted pink swirls on his side, and a big silver bow was knotted around his neck. "Looking good, Prince!"

Mia let out a little snort of frustration. "Rosie, you have to get him out of here!" she exclaimed. "We want to make a good impression on our visiting celebrity, don't we?"

"Celebrity?" Rosie perked up. "What celebrity?"

"Poppy Addison," Susie told her eagerly. "She's amazing!"

"Never heard of her." Rosie frowned. "Wait—she's not the actress from that new action movie, is she? The one with all the hair?"

Susie laughed. "No, she's a world-famous horse-woman. She's always getting interviewed about her riding, and they did a big feature about her on BBC News when she made the Olympic team."

"Hmm. A horse celebrity?" Rosie shrugged. "Not exactly Hollywood A-list, but I guess that's kind of cool. Maybe I can paint her into my masterpiece. When's she getting here?"

Mia's eyes widened as she stared at something over Zoe's shoulder. "Right now!" she exclaimed. "There she is!"

4

Celebrity Sighting

Zoe turned and saw Mia's father entering the yard. Beside him was a woman dressed in jeans and a red polo shirt. Her sandy-colored hair was cut in a neat bob, and freckles dotted her heart-shaped face.

"It's her!" Susie stage-whispered, looking awestruck. "Poppy Addison—in the flesh!"

Mia glared at goofy Bob and paint-covered Prince. "Get those ponies out of here!" she hissed. Then she pasted a big smile on her face, turned, and waved. "Welcome, Poppy!" she called out. "Sorry about the mess around the yard."

She rushed off to meet them. Zoe hung back with the others.

"*That's* the big celebrity you guys were talking about?" Rosie whispered, sounding decidedly unimpressed. "She's not exactly red carpet ready, is she?"

"Do you see any red carpets around here?" Zoe whispered back.

Jade giggled. "No way—if there were one, Bob would probably eat it."

That made Becky snort with laughter. "Yeah, he thinks anything red is edible—watch!" She grabbed a red lead rope off the fence and held it out.

Bob was nibbling at the rope when Mr. MacDonald led Poppy over. "Girls, I'm glad you're all here," he said. "I'd like you to meet my dear old friend Poppy Addison. I'm sure you've heard she'll be staying with us for the next couple of days."

"Brilliant to meet you all." The visitor's smile was wide and genuine. "I'm Poppy, and I'm so happy to be here."

"I'm Zoe," Zoe said. "This is my sister, Rosie, and that's Jade, and—"

"Oh, Zoe, don't bother!" Mia cut her off with a trilly little laugh. "I'm sure Poppy's tired after her long trip from the mainland—she'll never remember all those names." She patted Poppy on the arm. "In fact, why don't we take you back to the house to settle in and have a nice rest?"

"Thanks, Mia, but I'm not tired at all," Poppy said cheerfully. She stepped toward Bob, who was still trying to figure out how to eat the lead rope. "And who's this, then?"

"Oh, this is Bob," Becky spoke up proudly. "He's mine. Well, mine and my brother's. We share him. Which is just as well, really—there's a lot of Bob to go around, you know? Especially since we're always having to clean off his bum, or—"

"All right, Becky, that's fascinating," Mia interrupted loudly, looking alarmed. "Why don't you put Bob away now?"

"Oh, please don't." Poppy reached over and scratched the spotted pony under his thick mane. Bob grunted with pleasure, stretching out his neck and flapping his lip.

"Hey, that looks cool—can you get Prince to do that lip thing?" Rosie whipped out her pad. "I want to sketch him doing that."

"Oh, are you an artist?" Poppy asked, stepping past Bob to look at Rosie's pad. "How cool! I can't draw so much as a stick figure myself—they all come out looking like hobbyhorses." She laughed and winked at Mr. MacDonald, who chuckled.

"Yes, my grandmother was a talented painter, and I'm following in her footsteps." Rosie tapped her pencil on her chin. "Or should that be following in her brushstrokes? Oh well, I suppose my biographer can figure out how to word it."

"Hey, Rosie, maybe you should do a sketch of Poppy with me and Daddy to commemorate her visit with us." Mia smiled brightly at her father, then turned toward the younger girl. "That would be a great use of your talents, wouldn't it?"

Rosie looked intrigued. "I haven't really tried sketching people yet, but I'm sure I could do it."

Poppy was still studying Rosie's pad. "You really are quite good," she said. "That looks just like your pony. What did you say his name is?"

"Bob!" Jade blurted out in alarm.

"Really?" Poppy looked surprised. "He's named Bob, too?"

"No—Bob is trying to eat your shirt!" Jade dashed forward and pulled the pony away, just as he wrapped his lips around the hem of Poppy's polo.

"Oh, Bob!" Becky cried. "Did he get much slobber on you, Poppy? Sorry about that. If there's one thing Bob produces more than poop, it's slobber."

Zoe laughed. "That's for sure!"

Mia's cheeks were turning red, and she looked ready to explode. "That's enough!" she cried. When Poppy turned to her in surprise, she quickly took a deep breath and smiled. "I mean, wouldn't you like to meet Firefly, Poppy? I'm sure my father has told you all about him."

"That would be lovely, thanks," Poppy said. "See you later, Bobs."

"This pony's name isn't Bob, it's Prince," Rosie called after Poppy as Mia dragged her off toward the stable row with Mia's dad at their heels. Rosie sighed and shrugged. "Never mind, Prince," she told him. "Everyone will know your name once my paintings make you famous."

"I'd better tag along and help Mia with the tour," Susie said eagerly. "Maybe Poppy will want to meet Darcy!"

She hurried off after Poppy and the others. Rosie tied Prince to the fence and then wandered after them, sketching busily as she walked.

Zoe glanced at her friends. "Maybe we should tag along, too," she said. "If Jade and I can't ride in the clinic, at least we can soak up some of Poppy's words of wisdom while she's here."

"Are you sure?" Jade looked worried. "I got the distinct feeling that Mia wants Poppy all to herself."

"Yeah, she is acting a little weird." Zoe shrugged. "But that's Mia, right? She'll get over it."

"Good point," Becky said. "Let's go!"

When they reached Firefly's stall, the kind-eyed gray gelding had his head hanging out over the half door.

Poppy was patting him while Mia reeled off their long list of accomplishments together.

". . . And Daddy kept buying me more horses—there was one called Fletcher, and another called Raven, and then Sparkles," Mia said. "But in the end, I realized none of them measured up to my sweet Firefly. Did you know he was stolen by horse thieves last summer?"

"Really?" Poppy said. "I can see why they'd want him—he's truly lovely, Mia."

"That's not exactly how it happened," Zoe whispered to her friends, a little annoyed by how Mia was acting. "The thieves were trying to steal Raven! They didn't want Firefly at all—they took him by mistake!"

"Hush," Jade warned softly. "It doesn't matter."

Susie dodged around Rosie to join Mia and Poppy. "My horse is right over there," she said, pointing down the row. "Her name's Darcy. I'm hoping you'll be able to give me some advice—we've been working hard on our dressage, and I'm so looking forward to riding in the clinic!"

"Oh, brilliant!" Poppy beamed at her. "I'd love to meet Darcy. And I'm thrilled you're taking the clinic—I hope you all are?" She glanced around at Zoe and the others.

"Not me," Rosie said, never taking her eyes off her sketch pad. "I need to focus on my art."

"Bob and I will be there with bells on!" Becky assured Poppy. Then she laughed. "Well, not literally, of course. Although I suppose if I braided some bells into his mane it'd be easier for you to tell if his trot rhythm is steady—sometimes it's a bit hard to see, what with all the feathers on his legs flapping around . . ."

"No bells!" Mia snapped. "There's a dress code for this clinic, you know. If Bob is to enter, you'll have to clip his feathers and shorten his mane."

"What?" Becky cried in alarm.

But Poppy laughed. "Oh, no, I won't hear of it!" she exclaimed. "I'm looking forward to seeing Bob in the clinic just the way he is. Feathers and all."

"Oh. Good," Becky said, looking relieved.

Meanwhile, Susie had led Darcy out of her stall. Poppy let out a whistle and hurried toward her. "What a beautiful mare!" she exclaimed. "Have you had her long?"

"Oh yes," Susie said. "We've been together for a while, mostly doing show jumping but focusing more on dressage lately—Marcus says Darcy shows real talent for it."

Just then, Raven, who was another couple of doors down, stuck his head out and snorted, kicking at the stall door. Poppy glanced over at him.

"Oh my, this place is full of gorgeous horses, isn't it?" she said. "You should have warned me, Elliott!"

"This is Raven." Zoe stepped forward to rub her horse's dark, velvety nose. "He's the one Mia mentioned. He used to be hers, but now he's mine."

She smiled. The thrill she always felt saying those two little words—*he's mine*—still hadn't quite worn off.

"Raven's not entering the clinic," Mia told Poppy. "He's still rather green."

"Funny, he looks more bluey-black to me," Becky whispered.

Jade giggled. "Green means novice, Becky. Or beginner."

"We're happy to have all level horses and riders," Poppy told Zoe. She gave Raven a pat and peered in at him over the half door. "And this fellow is so nicely built—I'll bet he has lovely gaits."

"He does," Zoe told her. "I'd love to ride him in the clinic, but I can't afford it."

"Oh dear." Poppy looked dismayed. "But are all the rest of you in?"

"Not me," Jade spoke up. "I can't afford it, either. But Zoe and I are looking forward to watching. I'm sure we'll learn a lot that way."

"I'm sure you would." Poppy stroked Raven's neck, looking thoughtful. "But perhaps we can come up with another option."

"What do you mean?" Mia's dad asked.

Poppy smiled. "I've just had an idea," she said. "Why don't we have a contest—a way to win a free spot in the clinic? I'm sure I can get my teammates to go along with that."

"What?" Mia blurted out, looking alarmed. "But there are already plenty of people signed up to ride." She shot a look toward Susie and Becky. "More than enough, really. Besides, this is your job, not a charity, right? You can't just let everyone ride for free."

Poppy gave Raven a rub on the nose. "We can manage one free spot! Especially for a deserving Bright Fields rider, since the stables is being kind enough to act as the host for the clinic. Besides, it could be fun," she said, her eyes sparkling with excitement and her words coming fast. "Anyone who wants to try out can come up with an original dressage test showcasing whatever that rider and horse do best. Then when my teammates arrive, we'll hold a little horse show—best performance wins the free spot. What do you say?"

Zoe gasped. "Are you kidding? That would be amazing!"

"Beyond amazing!" Jade's dark eyes were shining with interest. "I'm sure everyone who's not already signed up would want to try out."

"Hold on," Mia broke in. "We appreciate your, um, generosity, Poppy. But really—are you certain you want to be bothered? I mean, surely your teammates won't want to help judge some amateur horse show the moment they arrive, and you'll have people pestering you the whole time you're here . . ."

"Oh, I hope so," Poppy said with a laugh. "I want to spend most of my time around the yard these next couple of days—I'd be happy to help everyone prepare for their tryouts. So what do you say, girls?"

"I say, three cheers for Poppy!" Becky exclaimed. "Hiphip . . ."

"Hooray!" Zoe and Jade cheered, with Susie and Rosie and even Mia's father joining in.

Only Mia stayed silent, glaring around at all of them—though Zoe noticed she pasted that wide smile back on the moment Poppy looked her way. *Oh well, guess Mia's not getting to keep the world-famous dressage star all to herself after all*, Zoe thought. But she could barely contain her excitement. This was just the big chance that she and Raven needed, and she definitely wasn't going to waste it!

An Awkward Turn
of Events

*O*h my, is that the time?" Mia said abruptly. "We really should head back to the house now, Poppy—Daddy and I have planned a lovely tea for your first afternoon here."

"Oh! Thanks, that sounds brilliant," Poppy said politely. "I'll see you all tomorrow, though, yes?"

"For sure!" Becky said.

"We'll be here," Zoe added. "Thanks, Poppy!"

"Good." Poppy gave Raven one last pat, then stepped away and glanced around at all the girls. "I mean it, you know—I love getting to know talented young riders. I'm hoping we'll all get to spend loads of time together these next few days."

Rosie looked up from her sketch pad. "If you're so

excited about spending time with us, maybe we should all come to tea with you," she told Poppy with a grin.

"Rosie!" Zoe exclaimed, horrified.

Rosie shrugged. "What? I was just joking," she said, rolling her eyes. "It's not like I invited us to sleep over at Mia's house or something."

"Oh, I wish you could!" Poppy said with a laugh. "I haven't been to a sleepover since I was your age—I used to love them!"

"Mia throws fabulous sleepovers," Rosie informed her. "Right, Susie?"

"Yes, fabulous," Susie said.

Mr. MacDonald chuckled. "Hey, if you girls want to have a sleepover, you're more than welcome. What do you say, Mia?"

"Don't be silly, Daddy," Mia said. "Rosie was only joking. Right, Rosie?"

"Yes, but if Poppy really wants to do it, I'm totally in," Rosie said. "You'll come, too, won't you, Zoe? You'll love it at Mia's house—it's super gorgeous inside."

"Um . . . ," Zoe began.

Poppy clapped her hands. "Oh, what fun! Please, do say yes, Zoe!" she exclaimed. "You can tell me all about your beautiful Raven then. And of course the rest of you will come, too? Please?"

"How can we say no?" Zoe said, trading amused looks with Becky and Jade.

"Good, it's settled," Mr. MacDonald said. "Just go check with your parents and grab your sleeping bags, then come on over."

"No!" Mia cried, a look of desperation in her eyes. At Poppy's surprised look, she gulped and added, "I mean, they shouldn't come right away. It's early, and, er, I thought perhaps I could take Poppy out for a trail ride after tea."

"Oh, double brilliant!" Poppy exclaimed. "What do you say, girls? Are you up for an evening trail ride?"

"Sure!" Zoe said, and the others chimed in to agree.

"Oh, but I didn't mean . . ." Mia gulped again, then sighed. "Never mind. I suppose we'll see you back here at six, then." She spun on her heel and stalked off in the direction of her father's car.

"Yes, see you in a bit, everyone." Poppy gave a little wave. "I can't wait to see this island from horseback again!" Then she and Mr. MacDonald hurried off after Mia.

"Wow," Jade said as she watched them go. "Rosie, I can't believe you just invited us all over for a sleepover at Mia's house!"

Rosie shrugged. "What can I say? I'm multitalented." She held up her sketch pad. "Speaking of talent, I'd better go work on my sketch. Toodles!"

"Yes, see you later," Susie added. "I'm off to give Darcy a full grooming before tonight's trail ride. I want her to look her very best for Poppy!"

She disappeared into her mare's stall. Zoe was still leaning against Raven's door, playing with the little whiskers on his chin.

"This is so cool," she said.

"What—that we're going to sleep over at Mia Mansion?" Becky laughed. "Tell me about it! I'd expect an invitation to Buckingham Palace first!"

"Not that—I mean the tryout show," Zoe said.

"I know, right?" Jade sighed happily. "It's like a dream come true—and just when I was sure I had no chance!"

Zoe gulped, suddenly realizing something. "Wait—so you're going to try out, too?"

"Of course." Jade's smile faded. "Oh, I see. There's only one spot . . ."

"And we both want it," Zoe finished. She sighed. "I want it a lot, actually. I didn't realize just how much until I found out about the tryout show."

"Me too," Jade said. "This clinic would actually be a really nice break from schoolwork. I've been working extra hard lately—there was that big project for my journalism class, and then my biology experiment. Now all that's done, it would be nice to put my focus on riding for once."

"I get that," Zoe said, feeling awkward—as if she was trying to take something away from one of her best friends. "But the thing is, this clinic is exactly what Raven and I need right now to challenge us and keep us moving forward. Especially since we started off so far behind the rest of you." She smiled as Raven nuzzled her hair. "Okay, Raven, *I* started off behind the rest—you were just naturally brilliant all along!" Jade cracked a small smile.

Becky was watching both her friends with concern. "So you guys are okay with this, right?" she said. "It's not going to be weird or anything with you two competing for the same spot?"

"We'll be absolutely fine," Jade said. "Competition is healthy, right? It pushes us to be better, and that's a good thing."

Zoe forced a smile. "Exactly. C'mon, we're Pony Squad. Things could never be weird between us."

Jade gave her a smile back, but Zoe couldn't help but notice that hers looked a little forced, too. It would take a little getting used to, knowing they were now competing against each other. But they would totally figure it out—right?

Tension on the Trail

A few hours later, Zoe was in the courtyard tightening Raven's girth. The place was buzzing with activity—several horses were tied at the rail, while riders dashed in and out of the tack room and the stalls.

"I wonder what Mia will say when she finds out practically every rider at Bright Fields has invited themselves along on this ride," Zoe commented to Becky, who was grooming Bob nearby.

Becky looked around. "Can you blame them? I mean, how often do you get the chance to go on a hack with Poppy Addison?" She shivered. "Pinch me, because I must be dreaming! Hey, stop that, Bob—I didn't mean you." She pushed her pony's head away as he nibbled at her back pocket.

Zoe smiled. "It's just as well that Rosie decided to skip the ride and just join us later for the sleepover. I'm not sure she's ever ridden in this big a group."

"They're here!" Susie called from her spot nearest the gate. Darcy was already fully saddled, but Susie was still fussing over her, brushing the mare's already gleaming coat.

Zoe checked Raven's girth once more, then looked up as Mia and Poppy walked into the yard. Both were dressed in breeches and boots, with their hard hats hanging off their arms by the straps.

"Everyone ready to ride?" Poppy called out.

A cheer went up from most of the riders. Mia's eyes widened as she looked around. Then she spun to smile at Poppy.

"Are you sure you want to ride out in this big mob, Poppy?" she asked. "I was thinking it might be more fun for you to take Firefly for a spin in the ring. He's really a fantastically well-trained horse. I'm sure you'd enjoy him. And maybe Daddy can come watch."

"Thanks, Mia." Poppy smiled at her. "But I do ring work all the time, and I'm dying to go on a nice hack out. It's how I started riding back on this island many years ago, and I haven't done it in ages—I can't wait!"

"Oh, I see," Mia replied.

Zoe quickly ducked her head behind Raven to hide her amused smile. It was pretty obvious that Mia was still trying to figure out a way to have the famous rider all to herself.

When she straightened up again, she was just in time to see Jade leading Major out of his stall. Zoe hadn't seen her since their conversation earlier, and for a second she felt a twinge of that awkward feeling that had sprung up between them then. But then Jade spotted her and waved, and Zoe let out the breath she was holding. What was she worried about? It was like she said: It would take a lot more than some contest to come between the members of Pony Squad!

"Why don't you ride out on Firefly, then?" Mia was saying to Poppy. "He's the best horse in the barn, after all—and you're our special guest."

"Thanks, Mia, but I wouldn't want to steal your horse out from under you." Poppy stepped over and patted Bob. "Although if this cute fellow is on offer . . ."

"Oh, do you want to ride Bob?" Becky exclaimed. "I'd be super honored! I mean, we might have to lengthen his stirrups a few holes, and I'd have to show you how to keep him from stopping to eat all the time, but if you're quite firm with him he'll sometimes even canter a bit, and—"

Poppy held up her hands to stop her, laughing. "Thanks, Becky," she said, her eyes twinkling. "But I was only joking. As I said, I can't take another rider's horse. I'm happy to ride whoever's available."

Marcus emerged from a stall just in time to hear her. He was leading a tacked-up pinto Cob. "We thought you could take Fletcher," he told Poppy. "He's Mia's old horse. He mostly works giving lessons now, but he's still got some get-up-and-go when a more experienced rider is aboard."

"Perfect." Poppy took the reins from Marcus and gave Fletcher a pat. "What a handsome fellow! It's lovely to meet you, Fletcher."

"But are you sure you really want to go out rather than schooling in the ring?" Mia squinted at the cloudless early-evening sky. "It looks as if it might rain."

"Well, this is England, after all! We can't let a little rain get in our way." Poppy laughed. "And yes, I'm sure. Schooling can wait until tomorrow. Riding is supposed to be fun. So let's go have some fun!"

"Whoo-hoo!" Zoe cheered. Becky joined in, but Jade kept her eyes on her horse, looking very serious and focused as she led Major toward the mounting block.

Zoe frowned slightly. "What's with Jade?" she murmured.

Becky heard her and glanced over at their friend. "I know that look," she said. "It's the same one she gets whenever she has a big test to study for or a project due or something. When I see it, I know not to bother talking to her—she won't hear me, anyway."

"What? Why?" Zoe was still watching Jade, who had paused to check Major's girth and pull down her stirrups.

"You know those things a carriage horse wears?" Becky put a hand on either side of her forehead to demonstrate. "Blinkers, I think they're called. They stop the horse from seeing anything but what's straight ahead. That's how Jade gets—super focused on what she's doing."

"Why now, though?" Zoe said. "She can't possibly be taking the tryout so seriously, can she?"

Becky widened her eyes. "Have you *met* Jade? She's the queen of taking stuff seriously!"

"But she doesn't seem that competitive usually." Zoe picked up Raven's bridle, which she'd hung on a post nearby. "I mean, at shows and stuff . . ."

"That's different." Becky shrugged. "Jade doesn't care that much about beating out other people. Just doing her best or meeting her own goals or whatever, I suppose. In any case, once she sets her mind on something, look out!"

"Hmm," Zoe murmured as she led Raven toward the mounting block. She gave him a pat. "If she's taking this trail ride so seriously, maybe we need to do the same. At least if we want to impress Poppy."

The group set out a few minutes later, heading across a big field toward the rolling meadows beyond, the setting sun turning the grass into a sea of gold. Jade was up toward the front of the group, right behind Marcus, Mia, and Poppy. Her posture was ramrod straight, and Zoe couldn't help wondering if she was trying to show off for Poppy so she'd do better at the tryout. Should Zoe do the same thing?

She was about to urge Raven forward when Becky came up beside her on Bob. "This is fun, right?" Becky said. "It's been ages since we did an evening ride."

"Yeah, barrel of laughs," Zoe said, tightening her hands on the reins as she saw Jade ride up beside Poppy. What were they talking about?

Becky shot a look forward, then returned her concerned gaze to Zoe. "What's wrong? You look weird."

"I'm fine." Zoe squared her shoulders, reminding herself not to lean forward too much, as Marcus often told her. Were her toes too far into her stirrups? She adjusted them and accidentally bumped Raven's side with one heel. He scooted sideways, almost crashing into Bob.

"Whoa." Becky grabbed Bob's mane to keep her balance as Bob sidestepped.

"Sorry," Zoe said to both Becky and Raven. Raven's sudden move had made her lose her grip on the reins. She shortened them, glancing forward toward Jade, who was laughing at something Poppy had just said.

"Seriously, are you okay?" Becky guided her left rein as Bob lowered his head toward a tasty-looking clump of grass. "You're not getting weird about this tryout thing, too, are you?"

"Stop accusing me of being weird!" Realizing her words had come out a little sharper than intended, Zoe shook her head. "Sorry. But really, I'm okay. Okay?"

"Okaaay." Becky looked dubious. "I'm just saying, you don't look like you're having much fun. And that's what this trail ride is all about, right? Fun!"

"You're right," Zoe agreed. "It's just that I really, really want this for me and Raven."

"And so does Jade," Becky reminded her gently. "Seriously awkward, huh?"

"Totally. And it doesn't help that she's been riding so much longer than me, and Major already knows how to do dressage . . ."

Becky nodded sympathetically. "Don't think about that stuff. Just do your best and I'm sure things will work out."

Zoe quickly did another mental check of her riding position. Not that it mattered—Poppy wasn't looking at her. She was still chatting happily with Jade up front.

"Don't worry, I'm definitely planning on doing my best," Zoe told Becky. "Better than my best—hey, easy, Raven." She clutched her reins even more tightly as her horse surged forward, shaking his head.

"Whoa, Raven!" Becky called.

But Raven was scooting to the side now, still tossing his head up and down. "Stop it!" Zoe muttered. "What's going on, boy?"

"He can probably tell that you're tense," Becky called. "You know, because of what we were just . . ."

Zoe didn't hear the rest of what Becky said. Because Raven finally ripped the reins loose and took off, charging toward the front of the ride.

"Hey! You're supposed to call out when you're planning to pass!" one of the other riders exclaimed, sounding annoyed as Raven charged past.

"Sorry," Zoe called back. "I didn't exactly plan it."

A few strides later, Raven caught up to the lead horses. "Whoa, Raven!" Marcus called out, urging his horse forward until he could grab Raven's bridle. "Easy, boy. You okay, Zoe?"

"Better now," Zoe said breathlessly, gathering up her reins again. "Thanks, Marcus."

Mia glanced over with a raised eyebrow. "Having some trouble, Zoe?" she inquired. "Or is that little move going to be part of your dressage tryout?"

Zoe gritted her teeth. "Nope, just a little communication issue. We're okay now." She shot Poppy a sheepish look, wondering what she was thinking. Had Raven's little freak-out made her question whether he was well trained enough to participate in the clinic? Or whether Zoe was a good enough rider to handle him?

"He's a spirited one, yeah?" Poppy said cheerfully. "That's a good quality in a dressage horse, actually."

"So's dressage training," Mia put in.

"Funny, but it's true, Mia," Poppy said with a smile. "Some of the most talented dressage horses in the world can be quite explosive and downright difficult to ride. Which can be a challenge, since the idea is to make it all look easy . . ." She laughed. "Anyway, he's calming down now, isn't he?"

Zoe realized she was right. While she was listening with interest to what Poppy was saying, Raven had stopped prancing and was walking normally again. "Good boy," she murmured, giving him a pat.

Just then, Susie rode up on Darcy. "We should show Poppy the tree where Becky thought she saw Ghost Pony that time," she suggested.

Mia rolled her eyes. "Don't be silly, Susie," she said. "Poppy doesn't care about some old fairy tale."

"Oh, but I do!" Poppy exclaimed. "When I was a kid, we used to have sleepovers in the loft at the barn and try to scare one another with stories about Ghost Pony . . ."

"Did someone mention Ghost Pony?" Suddenly, Becky and Bob trotted up to join them.

Zoe groaned, then laughed. "Uh-oh, don't get Becky started!" she joked, automatically turning to smile at Jade. How many times had the two of them tried to convince Becky that Ghost Pony wasn't real?

But Jade didn't seem to hear her. She was looking down at Major.

Zoe sighed and slumped in her saddle, barely hearing a word as Becky chattered excitedly at Poppy about the tale of Ghost Pony.

The group wound its way uphill toward the supposedly haunted tree. Halfway there, Firefly suddenly pricked his ears and snorted.

"What's the matter, boy?" Mia gave him a pat. "See something spooky up ahead?"

"Ghost Pony is back, perhaps?" Becky said.

By then, Raven and the other horses were on alert, too. "I see what they're reacting to," Marcus said. "A plastic bag is caught in the long grass, and the wind's blowing it about."

Now Zoe saw it, too. "It's not a ghost pony, or any kind of ghost," she told Raven. "You don't have to be scared."

Raven ignored her, flaring his nostrils and skittering to the side. "Hey, watch it!" Mia said as Raven bumped against Firefly, who spurted forward, shaking his head. He got a little too close to Darcy, who kicked out and tossed her head. Meanwhile, Marcus's horse snorted and pranced, and even quiet old Fletcher was moving sideways nervously.

"It's okay—I'll get it," Jade offered. "Major isn't spooked at all. Come on, boy."

She urged the steady ex–police horse forward. Major pricked his ears when they neared the bag, but he stood quietly while Jade dismounted.

"Easy, Raven," Zoe whispered as she felt her horse tense up beneath her.

"Pick it up slowly, Jade," Marcus called. "You don't want to spook the horses even more by making a lot of noise."

Jade nodded. Then she looped her horse's reins over her arm and stepped toward the bag. Seconds later, it was crumpled up in her pocket.

"Need any help remounting?" Becky asked. "I could get off and hold Major for you—Bob's nice and short, so I can get back on without help."

"Thanks, Becky, but I'm fine." Jade put the reins back over Major's head and stepped to his side. Zoe expected her to mount immediately, but instead, Jade checked the girth, adjusted the reins carefully on Major's withers, and finally lifted her left foot toward the stirrup.

"Nicely done, Jade," Marcus said once she'd remounted. "I was going to remind you to check your girth before you got back on, but you beat me to it."

Poppy smiled. "I see your students are well trained, Marcus," she said approvingly.

"Not all of us," Becky spoke up with a laugh. "The reason Marcus is so anxious about that is because one time I got off to move a branch off the trail, and when I tried to get back on, the saddle spun around and ended up under Bob's belly. Needless to say, I ended up on the ground."

Zoe laughed along with everyone else, but she was watching Poppy, who was still smiling as if Jade's remount was the best thing since sliced bread. Had that just won her a few more points toward that free clinic spot?

"Come on, Raven," she said, deciding to even the score. "Let's lead the way to Ghost Pony Tree."

She urged her horse forward. But when they neared the spot where the bag had been, Raven snorted and leaped to the side.

"Hey!" Zoe blurted out, barely keeping her balance. She'd lost both her stirrups in the spook and fished around for them while doing her best to stop Raven from wheeling away and bolting off, as she could tell he wanted to do.

"Easy, Zoe," Marcus called. "Just let him back away if he wants to."

Poppy nodded. "I think they're all still a little spooked and looking around for that terrifying bag."

Zoe glanced toward Poppy. Fletcher didn't seem particularly spooked anymore, though Firefly and some of the others still looked tense.

"It's okay, we can lead the way past," Jade said. "Major's not spooked at all—the others usually trust him to lead."

Becky nodded. "And Bob and I can bring up the rear. He's not afraid of the bag, either. I'm surprised he didn't try to eat it, actually."

"Cheers, girls," Poppy said. "Lead the way, then, Jade."

Once everyone was well beyond the spooky spot, Zoe relaxed her grip on the reins. "Good boy, Raven," she said. "We survived. Who knew a plastic bag could be so terrifying?"

Poppy heard her and chuckled. "Horses are funny, aren't they? They're all different—just like people." She glanced toward Jade and Major. "Thanks for leading us past the scary spot, Jade."

Jade blushed and looked pleased. "You're welcome, Poppy," she said. "It's all down to Major, really—he's amazing."

"Yes, he is." Poppy shortened her reins. "Now what do you say—anyone fancy a bit of a trot?"

When Marcus gave the okay, Poppy clucked and sent Fletcher trotting briskly forward. Zoe couldn't help admiring the easy way that Poppy posted along to the big gelding's trot, her hands and seat light and her legs never moving. Zoe had the feeling that Poppy could have convinced Fletcher to walk past the scary bag on his own without too much trouble. But it was also obvious that she was impressed by Jade and Major. Zoe wanted to be happy for her friend. But she also couldn't help but wonder: What did this mean for her and Raven's chances at the competition?

Sleepover Shenanigans

"More potatoes, Zoe?" Mia's dad asked.

"Sure, thanks." Zoe looked up from her plate and smiled as he passed her a platter. It felt a little weird to be here in Mia's fancy house, eating dinner off her fancy dishes in her fancy dining room. Mia seemed to agree, since she kept looking around with a funny scowl. Jade and Becky had been pretty quiet since arriving, seeming a bit awed by their surroundings. Rosie, on the other hand, looked as if she fit right in.

Typical, Zoe thought with a fond little smile, watching her sister chatter happily at Susie about her new painting career.

Despite her worries about the tryout, Zoe had to admit that she was having fun. The food was delicious, and the conversation was even better. Poppy had spent much of the last half hour telling stories about her competitive dressage career and also about growing up riding on the island.

"So tell me, Poppy." Mr. MacDonald served himself more peas. "You got to see our girls ride today—what'd you think? Is Bright Field Stables up to your Olympic standards? Anyone particularly impress you as a future superstar?" He turned and winked at Mia.

"Oh, Daddy." Mia smiled and shook her head. "Don't put poor Poppy on the spot like that. I'm sure she won't want to look as if she's choosing favorites."

Poppy laughed. "There's the same old Elliott—always Mr. Competitive," she joked. "That's why I could never get him to go riding with me, you see. He knew he couldn't beat me at that!"

Mr. MacDonald chuckled and held up both hands in surrender. "Guilty as charged," he said. "I never could sit on a horse without tipping to one side or the other. Good thing Mia didn't inherit my lack of talent, eh?"

"Yes, good thing," Poppy agreed, smiling at Mia. "She's a lovely rider."

Mia looked pleased. "Thanks, Poppy," she said. "And, Daddy, don't worry, we can't all be talented at everything." She turned back to Poppy. "So what did you think of Firefly? He's really something special, isn't he?"

"Absolutely," Poppy said, helping herself to another roll.

Mia shot a triumphant smile around the table. "See, Daddy? I told you she'd recognize a quality horse."

"Speaking of quality horses . . ." Poppy set her roll on her plate and turned toward Becky. "Tell me more about Bob. How long have you had him? Is it true that he's a hip-hop dressage star?"

Becky's eyes widened. "You heard about that?" she exclaimed. "Oh wow—I didn't think he was that famous off the island, but I suppose it's possible word got out via my blog, or—"

"No, Becky," Jade broke in with a laugh. "I told Poppy about it during the trail ride."

"You did?" Mia stared at her over the rim of her water glass. "Why?"

"Oh, I just mentioned that we Bright Fields riders already have some experience inventing our own dressage tests," Jade said. "I explained how Becky and I came up with Bob's routine, and how well it went over at the County Show."

"Don't worry, though," Poppy said. "I'm happy to help anyone who isn't as naturally talented at hip-hop dressage as Becky and Jade."

Zoe took a quick sip from her own water glass. Great. So while Zoe had been embarrassing herself on that trail ride by letting Raven run away and spook at bags, Jade had been impressing Poppy by talking about their routines.

Mia's mind seemed to be on the same general topic. "I've been thinking, Poppy," she said. "I still wonder if this whole tryout show thing isn't going to work out after all. Your teammates aren't going to want to spend their first day on the island watching silly hip-hop routines or whatever, not to mention what sort of novice horse-and-rider pair you could end up with in the end." She shot a quick look toward Zoe. "Besides, wouldn't it be better to keep the clinic more, you know, intimate? That way you'd have more one-on-one time with me and Firefly."

"Hey, what about the rest of us?" Becky said. "Bob and I will be there, too!"

Susie nodded. "And me and Darcy."

Poppy just chuckled and reached for the butter. "Don't worry, Mia, you'll learn loads—I promise," she said. "Having riders of varying levels is incredibly useful in this sort of clinic setting. The more novice riders can learn by watching the more experienced. And the more experienced get a chance to learn the basics in a more concentrated way than they might otherwise, which can only improve their riding as well."

"Oh." Mia looked unconvinced. "But still, are you sure about the tryouts? Quite a few riders from Bright Fields are already signed up . . ."

"And don't forget about the ones from Holloway," Mr. MacDonald added.

"What?" Mia sat up a little straighter. "Holloway?"

"Yes, your father invited them to participate as well," Poppy said. "I believe they have three or four riders coming."

"You didn't tell me that, Daddy," Mia said sharply.

"Didn't I?" Her father shrugged. "Sorry, darling. Must have slipped my mind. They're quite excited about the opportunity to ride with Poppy and her teammates, apparently."

Zoe traded an alarmed look with Becky and Jade. "Holloway, huh?" Zoe said. "Well, that should be interesting . . ." Holloway and Bright Fields had been rivals since long before Zoe's arrival on the island, and there was no love lost between the two yards.

"Holloway riders aren't allowed to compete in the try-out, are they?" Jade blurted out.

Poppy looked surprised. "Well, no," she said. "That's only for Bright Fields—sort of a special bonus as the host stables."

That's good, Zoe thought, trading a relieved look with her friends. As stressful as it was to compete against Jade, she could only imagine tossing a bunch of Holloway riders into the mix!

After dinner, Zoe and the other visitors laid out their sleeping bags in Mia's cavernous bedroom.

Zoe was surprised to see her little sister spreading her sleeping bag at the far end of the room, well away from the others. "Since when are you such a wallflower, Rosie?" she asked, wandering over. "I thought you'd want to be right in the middle of everything."

"I'd love to, but I have to sacrifice for my art." Rosie plopped a duffel bag on her pillow and started pulling out items: a sketch pad, a set of charcoal pencils, some paints, and even a collapsible easel. "I'm planning to sketch the sleepover, and this spot offers the best perspective on the scene. I think it'll be a nice counterpoint to my more outdoorsy works."

"Counterpoint? Perspective? Outdoorsy?" Zoe wrinkled her nose. "Who are you, strange artsy girl, and what have you done with my little sister?"

"Typical," Rosie replied with a sniff. "We artists are always misunderstood by the common people . . . and, okay, I may have done some Internet research last night."

She grabbed for a charcoal pencil, but accidentally knocked over the whole container. Most of the pencils tumbled onto the pale carpet.

"Watch it, you'd better not get Mia's carpet dirty," Zoe warned her sister, a little distracted by the sight of Poppy coming into the room. "You know she always likes everything perfect."

"I know. I'll get them." Rosie lunged for the pencils, but tripped over her easel and went sprawling. "Ow!"

When she sat up, several of the charcoal pencils were squashed where Rosie had landed. Zoe cringed as she saw the dark smudges on her sister's shirt—and on the formerly pristine carpet.

"It's okay," she told Rosie, who looked horrified. "I'm sure Mia won't be that mad. She has, like, a million maids, right? I'm sure they can clean it up tomorrow."

"No, I'd better get some paper towels or something. Be right back." Rosie dashed out of the room.

Zoe shrugged and tossed her sister's sleeping bag over the spot to hide it until she got back. Then she returned to her own sleeping bag, which she'd already laid out next to Becky's. Jade was carefully smoothing out the wrinkles in her sleeping bag on Becky's other side.

"Are you sure we should let Becky sleep in the middle?" Zoe joked, smiling at Jade. "She'll probably keep us up all night eating food and telling ghost stories, as usual. Then we'll be too sleepy tomorrow to come up with our dressage tests for the tryout."

"It's okay," Jade said without looking up. "I already worked out most of mine in my head."

"Um, not really the point," Zoe muttered, her smile fading. "But whatever."

That finally made Jade look up. "Zoe, what's the problem?"

Zoe responded before she could stop herself. "You're the one who's acting like a totally different person all of a sudden."

Jade blinked, looking startled. "What are you talking about?"

Becky had joined them and jumped in quickly. "She's just joking. Right, Zoe?"

But Zoe was tired of keeping her thoughts to herself. She and Jade were best friends. That meant they should be able to talk this out, right?

"It's like this tryout thing is turning you into a zombie or something," she said. "I thought we weren't going to let it come between us."

"We aren't," Jade said. "At least I'm not, and I thought you weren't, either."

Zoe shrugged. "You could've fooled me," she said. "I mean, we've competed against each other at shows before, and you were never like this—all intense and, you know . . ."

". . . Thinking I could beat you?" Jade sat up and folded her arms. "Is that the difference? Because you're right; I never expected to beat you at shows—Raven's the best jumper at the stables, after all. But this is different. I want to win. And I think I can."

Zoe's jaw dropped. "So that's how it is?" she exclaimed. "You don't even care how much Raven and I need this clinic? It's all about you, you, you?"

"Zoe!" Becky cried, looking shocked.

Zoe gulped, realizing she'd gone too far. But it was too late to take it back. Jade was already jumping to her feet and storming off across the room.

"Oops," Zoe said. "I should go after her, try to explain . . ."

"No, wait." Becky grabbed her arm before she could move. "Give her a second to cool off first. It takes a lot to get her cheesed off, but when she does . . ." She poofed out her lips and waved her arms, miming an explosion. Or maybe a volcanic eruption. Zoe couldn't tell and wasn't going to ask.

"I didn't mean it like it sounded," Zoe said, feeling worse by the minute.

"How *did* you mean it, then?" Becky asked. "I mean, you pretty much accused her of being all about herself and not caring about you and Raven at all. Or puppies or kittens or the Queen of England, for that matter."

"I did?" Zoe blinked, thinking back over her own words. "Oops. Maybe I did say something like that. But only because I really want Raven to have the chance to be in that clinic. It would be so good for him—for us." She bit her lip and glanced across the room at Jade, who was talking to Susie over near the window. "I know Jade would understand that if I just explain . . ."

"Don't worry, the good thing is Jade doesn't hold a grudge," Becky said. "Once I accidentally spilled hoof polish all over her brand-new breeches, and she forgave me after only, like, two or three days. Maybe four, max."

Zoe looked at her. "Not really the same kind of thing, Becky."

"I know." Becky patted her on the arm. "Just give her a few minutes to cool off, okay?"

Zoe sighed. "Fine. I should probably go check on Rosie, anyway." She told Becky about the charcoal pencil disaster.

"No, you stay here—I'll go find her." Becky hopped to her feet. "That time I spilled the hoof polish, I ended up learning how to remove pretty much any stain from anything. Trust me, I can help with the carpet situation."

"Cool, thanks." As Becky rushed out of the room, Zoe went to grab her overnight bag, which she'd left near the door. As she passed, Mia was showing Poppy around her room.

"Poppy, you can take the bed tonight if you like," she offered. "I don't mind sleeping on the floor."

"Thanks, Mia, but that's okay—I'll be sleeping in the guest room as previously planned." Poppy smiled sheepishly. "I've had a few too many falls and years of hard barn work to sleep on the floor, and I won't turn you out of your bed."

"Oh, are you sure?" Susie cried. "I was hoping we could talk about horses all night long!"

Poppy laughed. "A girl after my own heart! Don't worry, I'm happy to stay up late chatting. But we'll all want to get at least a bit of sleep—it'll be a long day at the yard tomorrow, yeah?"

"True," Mia agreed. "I want to give Firefly a good schooling to prepare him for the clinic. Perhaps you could give me some pointers, Poppy?"

"Happy to," Poppy said. "And of course I'll be available to advise everyone on putting together their dressage tests for the tryout."

"Good," Zoe spoke up. "Because to be honest, I have no idea how to put together a dressage test. Like, to start with, how long should it be?"

"Poppy meant she'd help you tomorrow, Zoe, not right now," Mia said with a tight smile. "Come along, Poppy—I told Daddy we'd join him for dessert in a few minutes. Maybe we should head back to the dining room now?"

"Thanks, but I couldn't possibly eat another thing, Mia." Poppy smiled and patted her stomach. "Dinner was so delicious that I had thirds!" She turned to Zoe. "Tell me more about Raven and what he likes to do . . ."

For the next hour, Zoe and Poppy talked about dressage, Raven, and all sorts of other interesting topics. A couple of times, Zoe was vaguely aware of Jade wandering past, sometimes glancing her way. But she tried not to worry about it. She was giving her space, just like Becky had advised, right?

Finally, Mia came over to interrupt. "Hey, Zoe, what happened to your sister?" she asked. "If she decided to go home or something, you should probably roll up her sleeping bag so it's not in the way."

"Oh. Um . . ." Zoe glanced around, realizing that Rosie still hadn't returned. Neither had Becky, for that matter. Where had they gone? "Maybe they got lost in your huge house," she told Mia with a weak smile. "We might have to send out a search party."

"Go on and find your sister," Poppy told her. "We can talk more tomorrow."

"Okay. Thanks, Poppy." Feeling a bit worried, Zoe stepped to the doorway and glanced out into the hall. A familiar laugh rang out just around the corner. "Rosie!" Zoe breathed, relieved.

A second later, Rosie and Becky stepped into view, both smiling. Rosie's art bag was slung over her shoulder, and Becky was carrying a plate piled high with cookies.

"Where have you two been?" Zoe demanded, hurrying forward to meet them.

"Oh, just having a spot of tea with Mr. MacDonald," Rosie informed her airily. "He adores my sketches so much I think he might just become my first wealthy benefactor."

Zoe raised a questioning eyebrow at Becky, who shrugged.

"What can I say?" Becky said quickly. "Your sister has talent. Excuse me—I'm under orders to deliver these to the party." She dashed inside with the platter of cookies.

Zoe followed. Mia was perched on the edge of the bed chatting with Poppy, looking like she was finally enjoying herself. Susie was listening from nearby. Jade was helping herself to one of Becky's cookies when Zoe entered, but she walked away as soon as Zoe approached.

"I guess that means you two didn't make up yet." Becky held up the platter. "Want one?"

"No, thanks. I'd better talk to Jade." Zoe followed Jade over to their sleeping bags. "Hey," she said. "Can we talk?"

"I suppose so," Jade replied cautiously.

"Good." Zoe took a deep breath. "Look, I'm sorry about earlier. You know my mouth works faster than my brain sometimes—that's what my dad says, anyway." She shrugged. "Listen, I know you're not all about yourself. You're the opposite of that, actually—the kindest, most caring and amazing friend ever."

"Oh. Thanks." Jade looked a little overwhelmed. "You're a great friend, too, Zoe. That's why I was so hurt when you acted as if you deserved that clinic spot more than I do."

"I don't think that at all," Zoe assured her, so relieved to be making up with her friend that her words tumbled out double fast. "You're an incredible rider, and you and Major are so great together—everyone says so!"

"Really? Thanks." Jade's expression relaxed slightly. "He's such a good horse, isn't he? And we've been working so hard lately—Marcus said our turns on the forehand the other day were nearly perfect."

"Uh-huh." Zoe gulped, thinking back to those turns

on the forehand—the ones she and Raven had never quite mastered. "We'll just have to see what they're looking for in those tryouts, I guess. Major's definitely got more dressage experience. Raven and I will have to hope they give us points for our special connection and how great we are together."

Jade nodded, then frowned. "Wait. Are you saying that Major and I don't have our own special connection like you and Raven?"

"No! I mean, well, yes, sort of . . ." Zoe laughed helplessly. "You know what I mean, right? Raven and I were meant to be together. But you and Major have a pretty good connection, too, even if he's not technically your horse . . ."

"A *pretty good* connection?" Jade put her hands on her hips. "Just come out and say it, Zoe—you think you and Raven should win that spot. You think you deserve it more than me because you're, like, soul mates or whatever. And because you're some natural genius rider and I'm just a hardworking girl with a well-trained horse to ride . . ." Her lip quivered, but her eyes remained fierce.

"What? I don't think any of that!" Zoe exclaimed, confused by how Jade was acting—and just when she thought they'd made up! "But that doesn't mean I'm not going to try my hardest to win that spot for me and Raven. I hope you're okay with that, Jade."

"Sure." Jade shrugged. "And I hope you're okay if Major and I beat you out for it—even if he's not *technically* my horse and we only have a *pretty good* connection." With that, she spun on her heel and stomped off.

8

Friends or Foes?

"Ready to go, Raven?" Zoe said as she buckled the nose-band on his bridle the next morning.

She led him to the door of his stall and peeked over. It was still early, but the yard was bustling with activity. Poppy and Mr. MacDonald were over near the tack room drinking coffee and chatting. Becky and her little brother, Ben, were trying to clean Bob's latest manure stain off the white part of his coat. Susie was brushing out Darcy's silky tail. Other riders were busy grooming or tacking up their horses. Rosie had come to the yard that morning, too—she'd set up her easel over by the office and was hard at work sketching. Jade was nowhere in sight. She and Zoe had pretty much avoided each other for the rest of the sleepover, and Jade had left early that morning, claiming she needed to rush home and charge her cell phone before returning to the yard.

Just then, Zoe's view was blocked by Marcus rushing past, carrying a large box. "Hey," she called to him. "What've you got there?"

He stopped and smiled. "Oh, hi, Zoe," he said. "I'm off to put up the dressage letters."

"Dressage letters?" Zoe swung open the stall door and stepped out, peering into the box. "What are those for?"

She reached in and pulled out a small metal sign, with two pointy legs and a square of white vinyl at the top with a big black letter B printed on it.

"They help mark out the dressage court," Marcus explained. "These letters are placed at certain spots around the outside. Riders have to transition between moves when they reach certain letters."

"Need any help setting them up?" Zoe offered.

"Sure, if you don't mind." He sounded grateful. "Looks like everyone will be converging on the ring any moment now, and I was supposed to have this done already but had trouble finding the box—so let's go!"

In the ring, Zoe left Raven tied by the gate. Then, under Marcus's direction, she helped poke the dressage letters into the ground while he set up a foot-high chain linking the letters together. The whole thing marked out a tidy rectangle within the riding ring.

"Wow," she said when they finished, stepping back. "So that's the dressage ring? Uh, I mean *dressage court*?" She imitated Marcus's British accent on the last two words, which made him grin.

Suddenly, Poppy hurried in, followed by several Bright Fields riders leading their horses. Zoe was surprised to discover that Mia wasn't with them—but knowing Mia, she was probably out shopping. Jade was in the lead with Major. Her eyes met Zoe's for half a second before skittering away.

Zoe frowned, not sure what to do. Should she try to talk to her again? Before she could decide, Becky appeared leading Raven. "I put his bridle on for you," she said, leading him over to Zoe. "You might want to check the noseband, though. He kept trying to pull away when I was doing it up."

"Thanks, Becky." Zoe quickly fixed the buckle on Raven's noseband. She pulled down her stirrups and was about to mount when she noticed Jade checking Major's girth. Zoe quickly did the same. The girth was snug, so she mounted and gave Raven a pat.

"Ready to do this, boy?" she whispered. "Let's get out there and impress the heck out of that Olympic rider, okay?"

She heard a horse passing close by and turned quickly. It was Major with Jade astride, and she was looking right at her. Zoe blushed. Had Jade heard what she'd just said?

Raven seemed a little tense at first, eyeing the dressage letters with suspicion every time they got near them. Zoe tried to settle him, but found herself distracted by the horses and riders whizzing past in all directions. It was worse than the warm-up ring at Junior Nationals!

"Heads up—passing on the inside," Jade sang out, sending Major trotting past without so much as a glance at Zoe.

Zoe frowned, noticing for the first time that Jade had braided Major's mane. "Who does that just for schooling?" she muttered. But she already knew the answer—somebody who wanted to win, that was who! Why hadn't she thought of it herself?

They were coming around toward the dressage court again. Once again, Raven tensed up when they got close, lifting his head and staring at the white signs and the lightweight chain swaying in the breeze. He tried to veer out away from them, but Zoe clamped on her legs and pulled on the reins to stop him.

"Lighten up with your hands, Zoe," Marcus called out from the rail. "Trust him!"

Zoe nodded, knowing he was right. She'd never been able to force Raven to do anything he didn't want to do. Things went much better when they worked as a team.

"Okay, Raven," she murmured. "We can do this . . ."

For a second, Raven lowered his head and trotted calmly past the dressage court. But then Jade and Major cantered past, swerving slightly and forcing Raven to take a step in toward the letters to avoid a collision.

"Hey, watch it!" Zoe exclaimed.

Meanwhile, Raven snorted and leaped forward, nearly crashing into Susie and Darcy. Zoe didn't even have time to call out an apology as she wrestled to get Raven back under control.

"Easy, easy!" Poppy hurried over, grabbing Raven's bridle and bringing him to a halt. "You okay, Zoe?"

"I think so." Zoe heaved a deep breath. "Um, thanks. He got a little nervous about . . ." She glanced toward Jade, now calmly cantering a circle inside the dressage court. Had she sideswiped them on purpose? "Um, he's nervous about the new letters, and probably also about being in the ring with so many other horses at once, I guess," she finished.

Poppy smiled. "See? I told you he wants to be a dressage horse," she said. "He wants the ring all to himself!"

Zoe laughed. "Maybe that's it."

"I have an idea." Poppy let go of Raven's bridle and stepped back. "Put him on a small circle around me—just walking."

"Okay." Zoe nudged her horse with her legs. He leaped forward, ready to move faster. But she managed to keep him at a walk, turning him to circle around Poppy.

"Good. Good. Just move with him—follow with your hands. Try to make his walk as pure as it can be . . ." For the next few minutes, Poppy talked her through the exercise.

Finally, Zoe turned to her with a smile. "He feels relaxed now," she said. "Thanks, Poppy! I never thought just walking around in a circle could be so interesting."

Poppy laughed. "That's dressage—obsessing over the simplest things!" she joked. "Seriously, though, never be afraid to return to basics when you're having trouble. They're the foundation for everything." She winked. "Well, that—and remembering that this is supposed to be fun!"

Zoe smiled sheepishly. "Yeah," she said. "Come to think of it, that might have slipped my mind just now."

"It's okay, just don't forget it again," Poppy told her with a smile.

Zoe smiled back, glad that Poppy had come to Bright Field Stables. Even if Zoe and Raven didn't win the spot in the clinic, she'd already helped them a lot.

Just then, Jade rode up. "Poppy, could you watch my test for a moment?" she asked, carefully not meeting Zoe's eye. "I could use your advice on how to work our first canter transition."

"Sure, Jade." Poppy gave Raven a rub on the neck. "See you later, Zoe."

"Yeah. Later." Zoe watched Poppy walk away with Jade and Major. "Don't worry, boy," she whispered to Raven. "We *will* win that spot. Just you wait and see."

❧

That evening, Zoe picked at her dinner, barely hearing Rosie's endless chatter about her new painting career. With Poppy's help, Zoe was pretty sure she'd figured out a good set of moves to show off what she and Raven could do. But she still wasn't sure it was enough to win that free clinic spot . . .

"Zoe?" an insistent voice broke into her thoughts. "Zoe? Zoe!"

"Huh?" Zoe blinked at Rosie, who was staring at her expectantly. "What'd you say?"

"What color is Fletcher's mane?" Rosie asked. "I was just telling Mom and Gramps that I want to try painting him."

"Oh. Um, I'm not sure—black, I think?" Zoe took a sip of her water. "So is that your plan? You're going to paint all the horses at the yard?"

"Maybe eventually." Rosie pursed her lips. "My current masterpiece is top secret."

Zoe's mother laughed. "She won't tell us, either," she said. "I can't wait to see it, whatever it is."

"Yeah. I'm on the edge of my seat," Zoe muttered.

Grampa leaned toward her. "You all right, Zoe?" he asked. "You seem a bit out of sorts tonight."

Zoe shrugged, fiddling with her fork. "Maybe a little," she admitted. "The tryout for the clinic is tomorrow."

"Oh yes, the dressage thing." Her mother nodded. "Aren't you excited? You and Raven must have a pretty good shot, right?"

"I'm not so sure," Zoe said with a sigh. "There are a few other people trying out, and every single one of their horses is older and more trained than Raven."

Her mother smiled. "Oh? And when has that ever stopped you two before?"

"I know, I know." For a second Zoe smiled, thinking about how far she and Raven had come. But her smile faded quickly. "That's not the only thing, though." She dropped her fork. "Things between me and Jade are super weird . . ."

"Jade?" Her grandfather looked surprised. "What do you mean? I thought you two were great friends."

"We *were*." Zoe shook her head. "But I might have accidentally insulted her a teensy bit yesterday, and now she won't even look at me!"

Her mother and grandfather traded a knowing look.

"She gets that from you, you know," Grampa said to his daughter. Then he winked at Zoe. "Don't fret, sweetheart. I'm sure you and Jade will make up soon."

"I hope so." Zoe picked up her fork and poked at her food. "In a way, it might be better if she wins that free spot. Or maybe if neither of us does."

Her mother patted her hand. "It'll work itself out," she said. "And even if you don't win that spot, at least you'll still get to watch the clinic. That should be an education in itself."

"Yeah, I guess so." Zoe sighed and pushed back her chair. "May I be excused, please?"

She headed upstairs, ready for this whole day to be over.

9

Bob to the Rescue!

The next morning, Zoe woke up before her alarm went off, wondering why she had butterflies in her stomach. Then she remembered—it was the day of the big tryout!

After showering and getting dressed, Zoe ran down to the kitchen, where her mother and grandfather were just finishing their breakfast. "I'm heading over to the yard," she said. "Where's Rosie? I was going to see if she wants to walk over with me, but I can't find her."

Her grandfather looked up from the newspaper. "Rosie? She left half an hour ago," he replied. "Said she had a lot to do."

"Oh?" Zoe raised her eyebrows. "Well, okay. Guess I'm walking on my own, then."

A few minutes later, she stepped into the yard, which was just as busy as the day before. Becky was rushing along with a bucket in her hand, but she skidded to a stop when she saw Zoe.

"Oh, you're here!" she said. "Rosie said you were taking forever in the shower, so you wouldn't be here for hours. Possibly days."

"I was only in there for, like, five minutes!" Zoe rolled her eyes at her sister's dramatics. "Where is she, anyway?"

"Not sure." Becky shrugged. "Probably working on her masterpiece, I would think."

"Right." Zoe glanced in the direction of Prince's stall. "Anyway, I thought I'd take Raven for a quick ride in the ring so he's not too fresh for tryouts this afternoon."

Becky nodded. "Good idea. Most of the others are getting ready to do the same."

Zoe headed to Raven's stall. He nickered when she entered, stepping over to nuzzle her.

"Hey, boy." She smiled, breathing in the warm smell of horse. "What do you say—feel like a little dressage today?"

A few minutes later, she led him out into the yard, fully tacked. Poppy was standing near the alley that led out to the ring, watching a couple of riders lead their horses past. She smiled when Zoe approached.

"I was just saying, my teammates rang and they're about to get on the ferry," she said. "I'll need to go pick them up shortly, but I've got a few minutes, so I thought

I'd watch your schooling for a bit and give you some last-minute pointers."

"That sounds great," Zoe told her. "Raven and I need all the help we can get."

Poppy chuckled. "Don't sell yourself short. You two are a great pair with loads of natural talent."

Out of the corner of her eye, Zoe noticed Jade leading Major up behind Raven. Had she heard what Poppy had said? Trying not to worry about it, she mounted and rode into the ring. A couple of other riders were already hard at work, and Marcus and Susie were watching from the rail, but Zoe did her best to ignore all of them. She turned Raven toward the far end of the arena, letting him look around as he walked. When he pricked his ears toward the gate, Zoe glanced that way. Jade was still fiddling with Major's bridle, and now Becky had appeared as well, leading Bob. He wasn't tacked up like the other horses—Becky was holding his lead in one hand and a grooming tote in the other.

Zoe rode over to them. "Hi," she said cautiously, looking more at Becky than at Jade. "Don't tell me you and Bob decided to enter the tryout? And bareback, even?"

Becky laughed. "Not hardly! Bob's so round it's a challenge to stay aboard him bareback, let alone trying to do dressage at the same time. No, I just thought I'd groom him out here so I can watch you guys."

"Oh." Zoe glanced at Jade. She was already turning to lead Major in through the gate.

Just then, Poppy hurried over. "Bob!" she cried. "Oh, darling, I've missed you so."

Becky giggled. "In that case, want to groom him with me?" she asked. "My rotten little brother was supposed to help get him bathed and ready for the clinic, but then he got invited to the movies and blew us right off."

"Are you kidding? I'd love it!" Poppy dug into Becky's tote for a brush.

"Okay, have fun," Zoe said. Then she turned Raven away from the fence and went back to work.

A few minutes later, Raven had just finished a nearly perfect trot circle when Zoe heard a commotion over by the gate. Glancing over, she saw Mia coming toward the ring leading a fully tacked-up Firefly. Mia was wearing a new pair of boots. *I was right about that shopping trip*, Zoe thought.

Becky looked up from combing Bob's tail. "What are you doing here?" she asked Mia. "The ring's already crowded with people warming up for the tryout—can't you ride somewhere else?"

"No, I want Firefly to get used to riding in a proper dressage court before this afternoon," Mia said, reaching back to pull down her stirrups.

"Don't you mean tomorrow?" Marcus said. "The clinic isn't until then."

"Oh, didn't I tell you?" Mia smiled and glanced around as if making sure everyone was listening. "I had a fantastic idea. Firefly and I are going to enter the tryout show!"

"What?" Zoe urged Raven closer, wondering if she was hearing things. "Why?"

"Yes, why on earth would you do that?" Jade spoke up, bringing Major to a halt nearby. "You already have your spot in the clinic."

"I know." Mia shrugged. "But why not save a bit of money on my entry if I can? Besides, it'll be good pre-clinic practice for me and Firefly, since we've been so focused on our jumping lately."

Zoe scowled, biting back what she really wanted to say. She was pretty sure that Mia was just trying to keep Poppy all to herself again by edging out the rest of them for that free spot! But she didn't want to say so in front of Poppy.

She shot an outraged look toward her friends, forgetting for a moment that she and Jade still weren't speaking. But she remembered when Jade kept her gaze on Major's withers rather than looking back at her.

But Becky widened her eyes and mouthed *OMG*! Zoe shot back a similar look, glad that at least *someone* knew how she felt.

"Really, Mia?" Susie sounded a little annoyed. "Well, in that case, perhaps Darcy and I should enter, too!"

Clearly sensing the tension in the air, Poppy set down the brush she was using on Bob's hindquarters and stepped forward. "Now don't look so serious, everyone," she said. "Anyone who likes is welcome to ride this afternoon. It'll be good practice, no matter what happens." She smiled around at all of them. "But don't forget, this is supposed to be fun, right?"

"Right," Zoe whispered to Raven. "I always have fun with you, boy. Now let's go show them how it's done."

For the next half hour or so, she did her best to focus on practicing the routine she'd come up with for the tryouts. It wasn't easy. For one thing, she couldn't help noticing that the other riders were all doing their best to ride near Poppy as much as possible—especially whenever they did something flashy, like a shoulder-in or a flying change of lead.

Then there was Jade. She seemed to be making a point of staying as far from Zoe as possible, even in the confines of the crowded ring. Zoe tried not to let that bother her, but she couldn't help it. Was it really worth winning a spot in the clinic if it meant losing her friendship with Jade? Then again, shouldn't Jade be wondering the same thing?

Most distracting of all, though, was Bob. Poppy and Becky kept giggling loudly as they worked over him—

painting his hooves with bright green sparkle polish; braiding long, fluttering multicolored ribbons into his mane; and even pinning a big fake daisy to the top of his tail. After a while, Poppy hardly seemed to look up at the riders in the ring anymore, let alone give them pointers . . .

It was obvious that Zoe wasn't the only one who'd noticed. Finally, Mia rode up to the fence and halted. "Poppy," she called loudly, "what did you think of the half pass I just did? Did you see it?"

Poppy looked up from tying off one of Bob's colorful braids. "Sorry, must have missed it," she said. Then she glanced at her watch and gasped. "Oh dear, I was supposed to meet your father by the gate five minutes ago!" She gave Bob a pat. "Back in a jiff with my teammates. Good work, everyone!"

Mia frowned as Poppy hurried off. "Well, that was fairly useless," she muttered. "Come on, Firefly. Let's get you a bath so you'll look your best for the tryout this afternoon."

She dismounted and led her horse out of the ring. Zoe decided she might as well do the same. She didn't want to tire out Raven so close to the tryout.

As she led him through the gate, Becky called her over. "Doesn't Bob look smashing?" she said. "It was Poppy's idea to dress him up a bit."

"Yeah, right," Jade said from behind Zoe. She'd just led Major out of the ring as well. "Leave it to Bob to distract her just when I could have used more advice on my canter transitions."

Becky rolled her eyes. "Don't take that stuff so seriously!"

"Easy for you to say," Zoe told her. "You already have your spot in the clinic."

"Yeah," Jade agreed, though she still wouldn't meet Zoe's eye.

"No, I mean it," Becky said. "Look at Bob. I mean, *look* at him! He looks completely ridiculous—even I can see that. And you know what? An Olympic dressage rider helped make him look that way!"

"Okay." Zoe tugged on Raven's reins to stop him from wandering off toward the nearest patch of grass. "What's your point, Becky?"

Becky sighed loudly. "Do I really have to spell it out?" she exclaimed. "You two are running around in a snit, and over what? This clinic tryout thing?" She blew a raspberry. "Come on, is it really worth it just to be in that clinic? Because Poppy—that would be the person *giving* the clinic—could tell you that's not what's truly important in life. You know what *is* important?"

"Fussing over Bob?" Jade guessed with the hint of a smile.

"Exactly!" Becky flung her hands out. "You could both take a lesson from Poppy, you know."

"Isn't that exactly what we're trying to do?" Zoe said.

"Not a riding lesson—I'm talking about a lesson in having fun!" Becky said. "A lesson in being more Bob."

Zoe stared at her for a second. Then she glanced at Bob—just as the daisy slipped loose and fell to the ground. Bob turned, nosed at it—then picked it up in his mouth, lipping it thoughtfully while pawing at the grass with one sparkly green hoof, his rainbow ribbons fluttering in the breeze.

Zoe couldn't help it—she burst out laughing. "Oh, Bob," she said. "You're so—so—" She paused, struggling for the right word.

"So Bob?" Jade offered, smiling now, too.

"Exactly." Zoe grinned at her. "So totally, completely, utterly Bob!"

Becky's eyes widened. "Hey, you're talking!" she blurted out. "Does this mean it worked?"

"The power of Bob, you mean?" Zoe joked. "Did it make us friends again?" She shot a look at Jade. "I hope so . . . did it?"

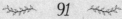

"Yeah." Jade shrugged, looking sheepish. "Sorry, Zoe. I guess I've been acting a little, um . . ."

"Non-Bob?" Becky suggested.

"Well, I was going to say intense." Jade smiled. "But non-Bob works, too."

Zoe smiled back. "I'm sorry about that stuff I said," she told her. "I didn't mean it. Or even if I did, I was wrong. Super wrong."

"Outstandingly, stupendously wrong," Becky put in.

Jade chuckled loudly. "It's all right. Becky can tell you I sometimes get tunnel vision when I'm working toward something really important or challenging."

"Like you have blinkers on, right?" Zoe winked at Becky, who grinned.

"Yeah," Jade said. "Something like that." She hesitated, running her hand down Major's neck. "It's like I start to wonder if I can really pull it off, you know? If I really have what it takes. And that freaks me out, and then getting distracted by freaking out makes me freak out even more . . ."

Zoe wasn't sure what to say for a second. Was smart, capable, logical Jade really just as insecure and uncertain as anyone else? It was a weird thought—but it kind of made sense, too.

"I get it," she told Jade softly. "And I'm sorry if what I said made you feel even worse. I mean, I want to win that spot, don't get me wrong—but in the end, it doesn't really matter as long as we're friends."

"Right." Jade smiled at her.

"Pony Squad forever!" Becky cheered.

Raven nudged Zoe sharply in the back, sending her stumbling forward a step or two.

"Okay, okay, Mr. Impatient," she told him with a laugh. "I guess this means you're ready for your bath now."

They all set off back into the yard leading their horses. "So you both looked good out there today," Becky said, sounding a bit tentative—probably afraid of setting off the fight again.

"Really?" Jade said. "I didn't think you'd noticed—you and Poppy looked pretty busy with Bob."

"Not that it matters, really." Zoe sighed. "Mia's probably going to win that free spot, anyway. Which is totally unfair, since as she told us, Poppy is practically part of her family."

Jade's eyes widened. "I know, right?" she said. "I could hardly believe it when she said she was trying out!"

Becky shook her head. "Besides, Mia could pay for all our clinic entries out of her pocket change, and still have enough left over to buy everyone muffins afterward!"

Zoe grinned, relieved to be talking with both her best friends again. Then she spotted Mia striding toward them. "Heads up," she hissed.

"Are you planning to stand there blocking the aisle all day?" Mia stopped and glared at them, hands on her hips.

"Don't worry; we're moving." Becky tugged Bob forward. "Come on, Bob. Let's put you away so I can help with the baths."

A half hour later, Raven and Major were both clean and drying in their stalls. Zoe stepped out into the courtyard and glanced around, rubbing her hands dry on her leggings.

Mia rushed by. "Don't just stand there," she snapped. "The other Olympians will be here soon, and this place looks a wreck! Grab a broom or something."

Before Zoe could even respond, Mia rushed off again. She glanced around. A couple of riders were still bathing or grooming their horses at the rail, and someone had left a wheelbarrow full of soiled bedding near one of the stalls. But otherwise the yard looked tidy enough to her.

Suddenly, Rosie raced over. She was wearing her artist's smock again, and Zoe noticed that it seemed to have more paint splatters on it than ever. In one hand was a palette smeared with various shades of brown, pink, and blue.

"Have you seen Becky?" Rosie demanded.

"Becky? I think she's in Major's stall with Jade," Zoe said. "Why?"

"No reason." Rosie shot her a quick smile, then scurried off.

Before Zoe could wonder what that was about, Mia appeared again. "What's wrong with you? I thought I told you to help tidy up!"

"And I thought your dad sold this place to Pin," Zoe shot back. "Which means you don't get to boss me around, Mia. You're just another rider here now."

Mia glared at her. "In case you've forgotten, my dad is the one who brought Poppy here," she said icily. "If you're going to insist on trying to horn in on the clinic, the least you could do is make yourself useful." She smiled insincerely. "I mean, I'd hate to have to tell Daddy you're not being a team player, Zoe."

"Is that supposed to be a threat?" Zoe demanded.

"Take it as you like." With a toss of her hair, Mia hurried off.

Zoe gritted her teeth. "Anytime I think Mia might be turning into a nice, normal, sane person, she has to go and change my mind," she muttered to Raven, who was hanging his head out over his stall door.

Just then, Jade rushed up to her. "Have you seen Becky?" she asked. "I haven't seen her in, like, twenty minutes, and she has my show gloves in her pocket."

"I haven't seen her in a while, either. Let's check in Bob's stall."

Zoe led the way. Becky wasn't in Bob's stall, though, and neither was Bob. At first Zoe assumed that meant Bob must have let himself out again, as he was prone to do—for Bob, stall latches were mere suggestions. But a quick search revealed neither the spotted pony nor his owner in the paddocks, the hay barn, the wash rack, or anywhere else around the yard.

"Did Becky decide to go off on a ride or something?" Zoe wondered.

Jade shrugged. "Who knows? She can be a little unpredictable, but that would be weird even for her . . ."

In a flash, Susie rushed into the center of the yard, pink cheeked and breathless. "They're here!" she called out. "Poppy's teammates—they just pulled up outside!"

10

A Dressage Disaster

Poppy's teammates, Keith and Fiona, turned out to be a little older than her—and a lot more intimidating. Keith was tall and lean, with broad shoulders and sharp blue eyes that seemed to take in everything around him. Fiona was very petite but sinewy, with deeply tanned skin and a voice that carried even when she was speaking softly.

Zoe watched from the doorway of Raven's stall as Poppy led them on a tour of Bright Field Stables. "And this is the tack room," Poppy said, pausing in the doorway.

"Very nice." Fiona's voice floated across the yard. Keith just nodded without saying a word. It was hard to tell what they were thinking.

Zoe decided it didn't matter. The important thing was what they thought of her riding—and of Raven. "We're going to show them, right, boy?" she murmured as he came over and nosed at her shoulder. Sometimes she forgot what an amazing horse he was. Why was she so worried about this tryout? They'd conquered bigger obstacles together before—she was sure they could do this. All they needed was to perform their best.

Just then, Susie stuck her head over the door. "Did you hear what Fiona said about Darcy just now?" she whispered, her eyes shining. "'Nice mare!' Can you believe it? An Olympic-level rider thinks she's a nice mare!" She rushed off without waiting for an answer.

Zoe smiled. "We'll have to see what they say when they meet you, Raven." She rubbed his nose, then let herself out of the stall, planning to change into her show clothes and then fetch Raven's saddle and bridle. The tryout wasn't due to start for over an hour, but Zoe wanted to make sure she was ready.

As she emerged from the restroom a short while later, now dressed in show clothes, she almost ran into Becky coming around the corner. Bob was right behind her, still decked out in his ribbons and glitter.

"Where have you been?" Zoe asked, reaching up to tighten her ponytail. "Jade is looking for her gloves." Suddenly, she remembered something else. "Oh. And did Rosie find you earlier? She was looking for you, too—no idea why."

"Rosie?" Becky widened her eyes, then laughed. She seemed slightly nervous, which Zoe figured was because of the important visitors. "Oh, um, yes. Yes, she found me."

"Good." Zoe glanced at Bob. "So are you planning to leave all those ribbons and things in for the clinic?" She grinned. "Not that it bothers me—in fact, I can't wait to see Mia's face if you do."

Becky laughed loudly. "We'll see," she said. "Anyway, I just brought Bob out for some sun. He's been in his stall for ages now."

Zoe blinked. "He has? Wait, but I looked there and . . ."

"Oh!" Becky broke in. "Look, there's Jade—I'd better get her those gloves!" She rushed forward into the courtyard, dragging Bob behind her.

Zoe trailed after her, a little confused. Poppy and her teammates were just returning from the paddocks. "So that's the grand tour," Poppy announced. "Great place, right?"

"Lovely," Fiona said politely. Then she glanced around the shed row, where several horses were looking out, including Raven and Firefly. "I'm looking forward to seeing what these young riders can do."

Keith nodded. "I am as well," he said. "It's an interesting idea of yours, Poppy, this competition for an extra spot in the clinic."

Fiona chuckled. "That's our Poppy—always creative."

Zoe noticed that Bob was stretching his head out to sniff at Fiona's pink jacket. "Look out," she called. "Bob's right behind . . . oops."

Fiona had just stepped away from Darcy and bumped into Bob, who jumped in surprise. His lead rope came loose, and he turned and ambled off.

"Bob! Stop!" Becky cried, running to cut him off.

He made a quick turn, dodging Becky as she tried to grab his lead rope. "I've got him," Keith exclaimed, hurrying over—just as Bob bumped into the overfilled wheelbarrow Zoe had noticed earlier.

"Oh no," she whispered as the wheelbarrow tipped and soiled bedding and balls of manure poured out—all over Keith's very expensive-looking leather loafers.

"Bob!" Becky cried in horror, finally managing to grab her pony's lead. "I'm so sorry, sir. He thought we were playing keep-away. It's one of his favorite games, and . . ."

"Sorry," Zoe said loudly, grabbing Becky to shut her up. "We'll just put Bob away and then come back and clean that up."

"Thanks, girls," Poppy said, while Fiona smiled tightly. Keith was too busy shaking the manure off his shoes to respond at all.

"Yikes," Becky whispered as she and Zoe raced toward Bob's stall. "It's a good thing Bob and I aren't in the try-out. Somehow I think Keith might hold that against us."

"Gee, you think?" Zoe rolled her eyes. "Let's hope it doesn't put him in a bad mood overall. I'm not sure he and Fiona are too impressed with this place, anyhow."

"What do you mean?" Becky swung open Bob's door and led him inside.

Zoe shrugged, glancing over her shoulder in the direction of the courtyard. "Just a hunch . . . Whoa! It's later than I thought. I really need to get Raven ready or we won't have time to warm up before the tryouts start!"

After a quick good-bye, she raced to the tack room. Raven's saddle, bridle, and girth were right where she'd left them. But something was missing.

"Where's his saddle pad?" she muttered, checking the floor nearby. "I know it was here after our ride this morning . . ."

She mounted a quick, frantic search of the tack room. Where could it be? She'd washed the pad especially for today and had been extra careful not to get it dirty that morning . . .

"Looking for something, Zoe?" Mia ambled into the tack room, a small smile playing around the corners of her

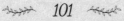

mouth. "They're about to draw for order of go—you don't want to miss that." She shrugged. "Not that I'm telling you what to do, of course. I'm just another rider here, after all."

Zoe barely heard her. "I can't find my saddle pad." She lifted a box of bell boots to check underneath. "The yellow one—have you seen it?"

Mia tapped her chin. "Come to think of it, I may have," she drawled. "There was something yellow in the muck heap when I passed just now . . ."

"The muck heap?" Zoe cried. She pushed past Mia and ran all the way there.

At first Zoe thought Mia had sent her on a wild-goose chase. Then she poked into the edge of the pile with her toe—and spotted a flash of yellow.

"No! No, no, no, no, no . . ." Zoe carefully dug into the stinky, moist pile until she could catch hold of a corner of the pad. When she pulled it out, she groaned. It was disgusting! Wet all the way through and smeared with manure and other dirt . . . there was no way she could use it now!

"But how . . . ," she began. Then her eyes narrowed. "Mia!"

Fury flashed through her as she remembered Mia's threat earlier. Was she really that determined to have

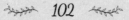

Poppy and the other clinicians all to herself? So much so that she was willing to sabotage her fellow riders?

Or maybe just me and Raven, Zoe thought, remembering how hard Mia had tried to discourage their participation from the first news of the clinic. And how annoyed she'd seemed by Zoe's reminder that she wasn't in charge anymore.

Just then, a loud shriek of dismay rang out from the main courtyard. "Oh no, what now?" Zoe cried, taking off in that direction.

She arrived to find Jade facing off against Mia. Major was nearby—with brightly colored paint smeared all over his rump!

"I didn't do it," Rosie cried, standing nearby clutching her palette and paintbrush. She stared at the people gathering from all directions, drawn by the ruckus—Becky, Susie, Marcus, Poppy and her teammates, and others. "I swear, I didn't do it!"

"Nobody blames you, Rosie," Mia said calmly, smirking at Jade. "It was an accident, that's all."

Zoe skidded to a stop in front of her. "Maybe the same kind of accident that made my clean saddle pad end up in the muck heap?" she demanded.

Mia merely shrugged, watching as Jade stared at Major with tears in her eyes. "I'll never get him clean in time," Jade moaned. Then she rounded on Mia. "You did it on purpose! You just can't stand anyone else competing with you for attention, can you?"

"What? Come on, don't be delusional," Mia exclaimed. "Accidents happen. You don't have to be so immature about it."

Zoe gulped, shooting a look toward Poppy and the other visitors. Keith looked startled, Fiona wore a disapproving little frown, and even Poppy seemed embarrassed by the scene.

"Now, now." Marcus stepped forward, waving his hands around uncertainly. "Let's just settle down, and—"

"Bob!" Zoe cried suddenly, spotting the pony wandering past. "How did you get out again?"

"I'm sure he unlatched his door," Becky said. "He does that, remember? It's like a hobby for him, really. Look, he already opened Fletcher's door, too—and now he's working on Raven's."

"No! Bob, stop!" Zoe raced forward.

But she was too late. Raven's door swung open—as Jade grabbed Rosie's paintbrush and threw it at Mia, who jumped aside just in time.

"Hey!" Rosie cried. "How am I supposed to finish my masterpiece now?"

Meanwhile, the brush went skittering across the yard—landing at Raven's feet as he peered out through the half-open door. He snorted at the brush, his eyes rolling and his ears flattening.

"Raven, stop!" Zoe lunged past Mia and Rosie, trying to grab Raven as he bolted out of his stall. He dodged her easily, rearing once before charging off down the alley leading toward the ring.

11

Pay It Forward

P eople were shouting and running in the yard, and Zoe could hear Becky and Jade calling her name and running after her, but she kept her eyes on Raven. "It's okay, Raven!" she yelled as she chased after him. "Whoa, boy!"

Raven cantered out the far end of the alley. The arena gate was closed, but that didn't slow him down—hardly breaking stride, he jumped clear over it, landing right next to the dressage court.

"Raven, stop!" Zoe shouted.

Her horse whinnied with alarm as the chain from the dressage court caught on his fetlock. He took off at a gallop, dragging the whole chain with him. Letters flew everywhere, and the chain broke into several pieces before finally coming loose from Raven's legs.

Zoe clutched the arena fence as Raven finally slowed to a trot, still looking a bit wild-eyed. Becky and Jade had caught up to her by then. "I'm so sorry, Zoe!" Jade cried. "I don't know what got into me—I wouldn't have thrown that paintbrush if I'd known it would set Raven off like that."

"It's okay; this is all Mia's fault, not yours," Zoe assured her. "She deserved to have that paintbrush thrown at her." Her mouth twisted into a half smile. "I'm only sorry you missed."

"At least Raven didn't lame himself," Becky said. "He's trotting around just fine."

"Yeah." Zoe gulped and shot a look at the remains of the dressage court, now scattered everywhere. "But still—look at this mess!"

Fifteen minutes later, things were mostly back under control in the yard. Poppy and her teammates had disappeared. Raven was tied at the rail between Bob and Major while Zoe did her best to brush off the dried sweat and dust from his wild run. Beneath his saddle was the only clean pad Zoe had been able to find—a brightly colored

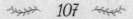

tie-dyed one borrowed from Becky. Meanwhile, Jade was scrubbing at the paint on Major's hindquarters. Rosie was hovering nearby, still clutching her palette.

"He looks a little better," Rosie said. "Maybe the judges won't notice."

Jade grimaced, scrubbing harder at a spot of bright blue paint on her horse's hip bone. "No, I've got to get him cleaned up."

"Give it up, Jade, it doesn't matter," Marcus advised. "You'd better just get his saddle back on. The tryout will start soon."

Jade dropped her rag. "Why bother to try out?" she said. "We won't have a chance looking like such a mess."

"Don't say that!" Becky cried. "You've worked so hard for this."

"Yeah, you can't drop out," Zoe added.

"I'm sorry." Rosie's dark eyes filled with tears. "This is all my fault."

Jade sighed. "It's all right, Rosie. It's just as well, really."

At that moment, Susie walked by leading Darcy, who was tacked up and looked elegant and spotless as usual. Zoe guessed that meant she'd decided to enter the tryout as threatened—probably just to try to beat Mia.

"What's going on?" Susie asked, glancing with confusion at Major's paint-splattered hindquarters.

"Mia sabotaged Jade's horse, and she's letting her get away with it," Becky told her.

"But we're not going to let that happen!" Zoe said, suddenly getting an idea. "Hey, Rosie, let me borrow your paint for a sec . . ." She grabbed the messy palette out of her sister's hand.

"What are you doing?" Becky asked.

Zoe grinned. "This." She smashed the palette against her clean shirt and jacket. When she pulled it away, it looked as if a clown had thrown up on her.

Jade gasped. "Zoe!"

But Susie laughed. "Here, I'll take that." She snatched the palette from Zoe and pressed it against Darcy's gleaming shoulder, leaving a large blotch of clashing colors.

Jade's jaw dropped. "Why did you guys do that?"

Marcus was grinning. "Solidarity," he said. "That's the true Bright Fields forever spirit!"

Zoe turned to face Jade. "So what do you say?" she asked. "If Susie and I can go out there and ride for a couple of Olympians looking like this, so can you. Right?"

Jade still looked stunned, but finally she laughed. "Right. Let's do this!"

Marcus whooped. Then he pointed at Zoe and Susie. "Go wash your hands first, though, you two," he said.

"Making a statement is one thing, but if you get paint on your reins it'll never come out."

"Oops." Zoe realized he was correct. "Be right back."

She hurried off with Susie at her heels. Halfway to the restroom, they passed the stable office. Loud voices were coming from inside.

"Hang on," Susie whispered, grabbing Zoe's arm. "What's going on in there?"

Zoe stopped beside her. She recognized Poppy's voice right away, sounding upset. ". . . And I'm not sure where this is coming from all of a sudden."

"It isn't all of a sudden," Keith said. "Fiona and I have been talking since we got here, and that little scene just now only reinforces our concerns."

"Yes. We're wondering if this idea of yours is worth pursuing after all, Poppy," Fiona added. "If these riders can't take themselves seriously enough to work hard and pay for a clinic spot . . ."

"Or even manage to prepare for this tryout properly," Keith added. "Well, we're wondering if we should just call the whole thing off."

Zoe couldn't listen anymore without speaking up. "No!" she cried, bursting into the office. "Please, you can't call it off!"

Poppy looked startled, glancing from Zoe to Susie, who had stepped in behind her. "Girls," she said. "I'm sorry you had to hear that."

"Zoe's right," Susie said earnestly. "You really can't cancel this tryout now!"

"Oh?" Keith looked down his nose at her, his mouth set in a disapproving line. "And why not?"

"Because we *have* worked hard—all of us!" Zoe waved a hand behind her to indicate the entire yard. "Okay, so maybe we aren't ready for the Olympics or whatever. Isn't that the point? You're here to make us better, right? And I guess we do need the help. At least I know Raven and I do." She clenched her hands into fists. "If you give us a chance, we'll prove to you that we do take riding seriously."

"I see. Thanks for your input, young lady." Fiona's voice was polite but cool as her gaze drifted to the mess of paint on Zoe's shirt.

Right then, Marcus poked his head in. Jade, Becky, Mia, Rosie, and several others crowded behind him, looking curious and worried. "What's going on?" Marcus asked.

"Yes, we heard the shouting," Mia added. "Is Zoe getting herself in trouble again?"

"They want to call off the tryout!" Zoe exclaimed, ignoring Mia's comment as she waved a hand toward Fiona and Keith.

Poppy stood up. "Nobody's calling anything off," she told Marcus and the others firmly. Then she turned to face her teammates. "You two just got here. But I've been observing these young riders the past couple of days. And you know who they remind me of?"

"A pack of rabid monkeys?" Mia muttered, though Zoe wasn't sure anyone else heard her.

"Myself!" Poppy squared her shoulders.

"You?" Keith sniffed. "Hardly."

"No, it's true," Poppy told her teammates. Then she glanced around at everyone. "I wasn't always famous, you know. I grew up on this island, totally pony mad but without enough money for a horse of my own—or even riding lessons."

"Really?" Becky said.

Poppy nodded. "So I worked at a yard even smaller and humbler than this, mucking stalls and stacking hay all day long—just for the chance to ride the scruffiest, naughtiest ponies they had. I never thought I'd get anywhere, and there was a lot of hard work and grime and sweat and even a broken bone or two involved." She smiled. "But it was the best fun I ever had!"

"What happened?" Zoe asked her. "How'd you go from that to, you know—you?"

"A trainer spotted me riding across the moors." Poppy grinned. "Actually, a rather wild young pony was running away with me at the time . . ."

"Been there," Zoe put in, thinking back to some of her earliest rides on Raven.

Poppy laughed. "Anyway, that trainer took me under his wing, brought me to his much nicer stables, gave me opportunities I never thought I'd have . . . and the rest is history."

"Wow," Rosie said. "They should make a movie about you! I know some people back in LA—we should talk."

That made everyone laugh—even Fiona and Keith. "So I suppose I see myself in this Bright Fields gang," Poppy went on, smiling as she glanced around at the group. "They have their hearts in the right place. They know how to have fun and goof off, but they also work hard. And I want to give them a chance like I was lucky enough to get."

"Pay it forward," Zoe murmured, remembering a phrase her father liked to use.

Poppy heard her and nodded. "Pay it forward," she echoed. "I like that."

Keith sighed. "Oh, Poppy, you're such a soft touch." His face cracked into a smile. "Fortunately for you, so am I."

"And me," Fiona added with a chuckle. "All right, let's draw spots for the tryout."

Zoe blew out a sigh of relief. She and Raven still had a chance . . .

"Wait," Mia spoke up. "Are you sure we still have time for this? I mean, I've been so busy cleaning up after all these disasters that I haven't even had a chance to change into my show clothes yet!" She shot the older riders an ingratiating smile. "That's why what Poppy just said about working hard really resonated with me."

"Never mind, Mia," Susie said. "Whenever we go shopping, you're always saying you can try on six outfits in the time it takes me to try one. You'll be show ready in no time."

Mia shot her a glare. "Okay, but what about the dressage court? Raven completely obliterated it—we'd need to set it up again."

"Ah, I'd nearly forgotten about that," Poppy said. "Thanks, Mia. If you don't mind taking care of that, I know we'd all be terribly grateful."

"Me?" Mia looked startled. "Wait, but I, um . . ."

"Yes, thanks, Mia." Marcus was clearly trying to hide a smile. "Given that you haven't changed into your show clothes yet, you're the perfect person to do it."

Susie didn't even try to hide her smile. "Especially since you're such a hard worker."

Mia sputtered for a moment. But after a raised eyebrow from Keith, she finally stalked off toward the ring.

"Good, that's sorted, then." Poppy checked her watch as she led the others out into the yard. "We should probably wait until Mia returns to draw for the tryout order. In the meantime, if no one minds, there's one horse here I've been dying to take for a spin . . ."

"Well, it seems we have a few minutes to spare." Fiona glanced around, her gaze settling briefly on Darcy, then Raven, and finally Firefly. "Which horse did you want to try, Poppy?"

Zoe held her breath. Was it Raven? *If so, you'd better behave, boy*, she thought, glancing at him.

But then she noticed Poppy walking in the other direction. Straight toward . . .

"Bob!" Becky cried happily. "I knew it! Nobody can resist his charms."

Keith and Fiona traded a surprised look. But Becky was already rushing off to fetch Bob's saddle and bridle.

"She's right, you know," Zoe told Jade with a smile. "Nobody can resist the power of Bob."

Jade laughed. "Too right. Come on, let's go help get him saddled."

A few minutes later, a sweaty, disheveled, and grumpy-looking Mia glanced up in surprise when Poppy rode into the ring on Bob. Only about half the chain was back in place, and none of the letters.

It would have been funny if she didn't look so pitiful. Zoe sighed. "Come on," she said, nudging Jade in the ribs. "Let's go help her."

As the three of them quickly put the dressage court back together, Zoe kept one eye on Poppy and Bob. "If he starts to slow down, you'll need to loosen your reins," Becky called out at one point. "It also helps if you sing him a happy song and rub his withers now and then. If you do that, he'll do almost anything you like. Almost. Usually."

Zoe grinned at Jade. "Look at that. Becky's giving a lesson to an Olympic-level rider."

"An Olympic-level rider who's riding Bob," Jade corrected. "That makes all the difference!"

12

The Moment of Truth

Zoe drew the last spot out of the nine riders competing in the tryout. "Great," she said with a wry smile. "That gives me plenty of time to get extra nervous."

Poppy chuckled. "You'll be fine, Zoe," she said. "Now, can we fetch a couple of chairs for our two esteemed judges?"

"Yes, and a table for taking notes," Fiona said.

"Sorry, we should have thought of that," Marcus said, already hurrying toward the office. "There's a folding table in here," he called over his shoulder. "Someone fetch the two chairs from the tack room."

"Just two?" Zoe asked Poppy. "Aren't you judging, too?"

Poppy shook her head. "That wouldn't be fair—I've been acting as your trainer these past two days, sort of, and I helped you come up with your tests. But don't worry, Fiona and Keith are more than capable of judging without my help." She winked at her teammates.

Zoe glanced toward Jade and Mia as they realized the same thing—it didn't matter after all what anyone had done to impress Poppy in the past few days.

Since she wouldn't be riding for a while, Zoe left Raven in his stall and walked out to watch the early tests. Susie had drawn the first spot, and she looked a bit nervous as she rode Darcy into the dressage court. But once they began their test, both horse and rider were all business.

"Wow, she's really showing off what they can do," Becky commented halfway through. She was watching with Zoe, though Jade had stayed behind to get Major ready, since they would be riding second.

Zoe just nodded. Susie's test was really impressive. She didn't just show off Darcy's gaits and transitions, but also her training—there were a couple of leg yields, a turn on the forehand, and several other moves that Zoe didn't know the names of but that brought applause from Poppy and some of the other riders.

When she finished, the judges smiled and nodded at her before lowering their heads to take notes. Their table and chairs were set up just outside the far end of the dressage court, giving them a great view down the center line.

Zoe was pretty sure that even Keith and Fiona had forgotten about the paint on Darcy's coat once they'd seen what she and Susie could do.

"Okay, that test is going to be hard to beat," Zoe muttered, feeling her optimism waver slightly.

"Never mind, Zoe." Becky squeezed her arm. "This is supposed to be fun, remember?"

Just then, Jade rode in. "Looks like she's ready to rumble," Zoe said.

Jade rode back and forth near the entrance to the dressage court, waiting for the judges to ring the bell on their table. That was the signal for riders to begin their test.

As soon as the bell rang, Jade pulled Major around and trotted him in through the opening in the chain. She began her test by riding straight up the center line—at least that was what Zoe knew she meant to do. Halfway there, Major suddenly lifted his head and skittered sideways a few steps. Jade got him back under control quickly, but Becky grimaced.

"Oh no. She'll hate making a mistake right off the bat," she said.

Zoe nodded, holding her breath as the pair rounded the corner and started their first trot circle. She felt as if she didn't breathe again until Jade's test was over.

"Nice recovery," she commented then. "She didn't let that mistake at the beginning mess her up."

"That's our Jade!" Becky said with a smile.

When Jade rode out of the ring, Zoe and Becky hurried over. "Great ride!" Becky said.

"Thanks, but it really wasn't," Jade said.

"No, you guys were really good," Zoe said, giving Major a pat. "You couldn't help it if Major took a funny step or whatever."

Jade sighed and slumped in the saddle. "Thanks, Zoe," she said with a grimace. "But it was my fault, not Major's. Poppy and Marcus both reminded me to ride all around the court so he could get a look at the judges' table, but I forgot and stayed down at the other end." She shrugged. "Plus, I was maybe a little tense . . ."

"You?" Becky exclaimed with a grin. "Never!"

Jade finally cracked a smile. "Yes. I suppose feeling me so nervous made him wonder if he should be nervous, too. So when we got close to the table, he spooked. That's all." She glanced at Zoe. "And we both know Major isn't the spooked type. So make sure you give Raven a good look at the judges before your test."

"Thanks, Jade." Zoe reached up and grabbed her hand. "I appreciate that. And you."

Jade smiled and squeezed Zoe's hand. "You're welcome."

Zoe felt her heart lifting. It was *so* much better when the whole Pony Squad was getting along!

Soon, it was Mia's turn. "Wow, she looks confident," Becky whispered as Mia rode into the ring.

"As usual," Zoe whispered back.

She held her breath as Mia began her test. Firefly seemed to dance around the dressage court, not putting a hoof wrong that Zoe could see. When they finished, the judges looked impressed.

"Wow," Zoe said. "That was just as good as Susie's test, right?"

Becky shrugged. "I'm no dressage Olympian, but I liked Jade's best so far." She poked Zoe on the shoulder. "But never mind—shouldn't you be getting Raven bridled and warmed up?"

Zoe realized she was right. Her turn would be coming up in just a few minutes!

After they were all ready to go, Zoe took a few deep breaths as she rode down the alley toward the ring. "Okay, Raven, we've got this," she whispered.

The judges were still scribbling their notes about the previous rider as she rode into the ring. Remembering

what Jade had said about Major getting nervous, Zoe walked Raven around the dressage court toward the far end. He snorted and pricked his ears when he spotted the judges' table.

"It's okay, boy. It's nothing scary." Zoe patted him, then rode around behind the table, letting Raven check it out from every angle. At first he stayed on his toes with his head up. But after a few times past, he sighed and seemed to decide it wasn't anything to worry about after all.

Zoe glanced toward her friends, who were watching from the rail along with Poppy, Marcus, and some of the other riders.

Thanks, Jade, Zoe thought gratefully.

Then she blinked as Fiona rang the bell. It was go time!

Raven trotted up the center line as if he'd been doing it all his life, barely flicking an ear toward the judges. He felt relaxed and focused—Zoe barely had to think about a transition or a turn before he was doing it. Halfway through the test, she'd planned a leg yield along one long side.

She glanced over, gauging how far they were from the chain. As she did, she caught a flash of movement outside the ring. It was Rosie—she was sneaking around the corner clutching something large and white in both arms.

What is she up to now? Zoe wondered. *Tell me she's not planning to unveil her secret masterpiece in the middle of my tryout . . .*

Suddenly, she realized that Raven was still moving sideways. "Oops!" she whispered, realizing they'd gone too far—and were about to hit the chain!

She panicked, picturing the chain getting caught up around his legs again, causing him to buck or bolt . . .

Pulling the reins to the side, she stopped his sideways movement just in time. But he tossed his head in protest to the abrupt aid, snorting and spinning in place and threatening to rear.

Easy, boy, Zoe thought, quickly adjusting her grip on the reins. *It's okay. We've got this.*

He tossed his head once more, then settled quickly. She turned him back onto the proper track, trotting the rest of the way down the long side and then picking up a canter as planned.

The rest of the test went well. But Zoe couldn't help being disappointed in herself. How could she have allowed herself to get distracted like that? Now there was no way she and Raven would be able to beat out Susie or Mia.

"Oh my gosh, I'm so nervous!" Becky clutched Jade's arm. "They're taking forever to decide!" The three friends were in the courtyard, along with most of the other competitors, awaiting the tryout results.

Zoe glanced up from brushing Raven's tail. "What do you have to be nervous about?" she asked with a smile. "You're not even competing today."

"No, but my two best friends are!" Becky exclaimed. "That's even worse!"

Jade laughed. "I know what you mean." She smiled at Zoe. "Good luck, Zoe."

"You too." Zoe gave her a fist bump. Then she sighed. "But I think we both know what's going to happen."

All three of them turned to watch Mia as she sauntered across the yard, looking every bit as if she'd already won. "Maybe Susie will beat her," Becky said hopefully. "Fiona really seemed to like Darcy, right? Paint or no paint?"

"Ssh!" Jade said. "Here comes Poppy."

"They should have a decision soon," Poppy told the girls. "And before you ask—I have no idea who they're going to pick. I left it all up to them." She smiled at Zoe and Jade. "But you both rode very well today. Whatever happens, I'm glad I got the chance to work with you."

"Us too," Zoe said. "And whatever happens, we'll be at that clinic tomorrow—even if we're just watching."

"Right," Jade agreed.

"Wonderful." Poppy smiled at them. "You can learn loads that way. Especially if you take notes."

She went on to give them a few other tips about getting the most out of the clinic as spectators. As she listened, Zoe found herself thinking how happy she was that Poppy had come to the yard a couple of days early—getting to know her had been truly inspiring.

"Hey," Jade broke into her thoughts. "What's Rosie doing?"

Zoe's sister had just come into the yard. She was clutching a large art canvas carefully in front of her. A piece of cloth was draped over it. Zoe was pretty sure that was what she'd seen her carrying earlier.

"Is that the canvas she's been working on?" Jade asked.

"You mean her masterpiece painting of Prince?" Zoe shrugged. "Probably."

Rosie skipped toward them. "Hey, Poppy!" she called out. "Do you have a second?"

"Sure." Poppy shot a look toward the two judges, who were still bent over their score sheets. "What's up, Rosie?"

Rosie grinned at her. "Mr. MacDonald and I came up with a fabulous idea the other night over tea," she announced. "It's a thank-you gift for you coming and teaching these guys." She held the fabric-draped canvas toward her. "Voilà! My masterpiece!"

"Is it one of your paintings? Thanks, Rosie," Poppy said.

"Oh!" Mia hurried over. "Rosie, did you follow my advice about the portrait of Poppy and Daddy and me?" She shot a smile at Poppy. "Isn't that sweet!"

"Um, not exactly," Rosie told Mia. "We had a better idea."

Zoe traded a quick, horrified look with Jade. Then she held her breath, hoping that Poppy would be polite about whatever childish stick-figure painting of Prince that Rosie had just presented to her.

Poppy flipped the fabric off the painting. It was facing away from Zoe, so she couldn't see it at first. But she could see the expression of surprised delight that lit up Poppy's face.

"Oh, brilliant!" Poppy cried with a laugh. "I love it, Rosie!"

Suddenly, Becky started to giggle. "We knew you would!" she said.

Zoe stared at her, suddenly realizing that Becky had been part of that tea with Mia's dad at the sleepover, too. What sort of crazy plan had she and Rosie concocted?

Poppy flipped around the painting so everyone could see it.

"Oh!" Jade cried. "It's Bob!"

Susie gasped. "And *us!*"

Zoe stared at the painting, impressed. It *was* Bob—there was no mistaking it. Rosie had done a wonderful job of capturing his shagginess, his floppy mane, and even his personality. The colors were bright, bold, and beautiful, just like Bob himself. Sitting on his back was a smiling Poppy. And surrounding the two of them on all sides were Becky, Jade, Zoe, Marcus, Susie, and Mia.

"Sorry if I missed anyone." Rosie glanced out at the crowd and shrugged. "Bob takes up a lot of space in the painting."

Becky laughed. "Bob takes up a lot of space, *period*!"

"Wow," Zoe said, still staring at her sister's painting. Her masterpiece. "You did that in just a couple of days?"

"What can I say?" Rosie shrugged. "It's a gift."

"Yeah." Zoe smiled at her. "It's really good." Then she sighed. "At least someone in this family is talented."

"Huh?" Rosie blinked at her. "What's that supposed to mean?"

"Nothing." Zoe shook off her fleeting gloom, determined not to feel sorry for herself and ruin this moment

for her sister. So what if she and Raven wouldn't be riding in the clinic? She could still learn a lot, as Poppy had said. "I'm just saying you take after Grandma," she told her sister. "And you're awesome."

Right then, Fiona cleared her throat loudly as she and Keith stepped toward the center of the yard. "We have our decision," Fiona announced. "If you'll all gather around, please?"

"Oh good." Mia hurried forward, smiling. Susie was right at her heels.

Zoe made her way toward the judges more slowly. She steeled herself for Mia's smirk of triumph . . . or Susie's smile of joy. Which one would the judges pick?

"We've taken the liberty of creating our own standard of judging for today's tryout," Fiona began. "It was inspired by Poppy's little speech earlier."

Zoe traded a confused look with her friends. What did that mean?

"Yes," Keith said. "Instead of simply choosing the rider with the best score, we've opted to disqualify anyone who was already entered in the clinic so as to offer the free spot to a rider who otherwise wouldn't have a chance to get in."

"What?" Mia cried, while Susie and several of the others looked surprised.

"Yes." Fiona smiled. "Poppy reminded us that we've all had people help us along the way. We want to pay it forward."

"Wonderful!" Poppy exclaimed, clapping her hands. Marcus grinned and joined in, and soon the entire yard was applauding.

Well, *almost* the entire yard. When Zoe glanced at Mia, she was glowering at the judges, her hands at her sides. Susie, however, looked as happy about the judges' announcement as everyone else.

"All right, all right." Keith held up a hand for quiet. "Let's get right to it. As I said, we've chosen the best rider from among the rest of the group."

"Or, rather, the best *riders*," Fiona added with a smile. "We're pleased to announce that today's winners are—Zoe and Raven, and Jade and Major!"

13

Winners Take All

The day of the clinic, Zoe felt as if she barely stopped moving from the moment her feet hit the floor getting out of bed. There was so much to do! She still could hardly believe that she and Raven would be riding in the dressage clinic after all. But since they were, she wanted both of them to look perfect. She arrived at the yard early and gave Raven a bath, then left him drying in the sun while she cleaned her tack.

She was polishing her stirrups when Jade rushed in, looking pale and frantic. "I can't find my girth," she exclaimed. "And I think the sole of my boot is coming loose, and Major just coughed, and I think I might be getting a stomachache, and—"

"Jade! Jade! Chill!" Zoe hopped to her feet and hurried over to grab her friend by both arms. "Breathe, girl!"

Jade took a deep breath. "Sorry," she said. "I guess I'm just a little nervous. I mean—Olympians! Right?"

"Yeah." Zoe smiled at her. "Olympians that you rode in front of yesterday. Remember?"

"I know, but this is different." Jade chewed her lower lip. "Anyway, I know you're busy. Don't stop your tack cleaning on my account."

"Are you kidding?" Zoe slung her arm around Jade's shoulders. "You're my friend. If you need me to drop everything and give you a pep talk, that's what I'm going to do. I mean, that's what friends are for, right?"

Finally, Jade smiled, though it looked a little shaky. "Right. Thanks, Zoe."

"Hey! There you are," Becky cried, rushing in. "I need your help with something."

"Let me guess," Zoe said. "Bob rolled in the muck heap again, and you need our help giving him a bath?"

"Or he ate his bridle, so you want us to help you find one to use?" Jade added.

"Or he chewed up Keith's shoes and we have to run to the shops and buy him a new pair?" Zoe guessed with a grin.

Becky was laughing by then. "No, none of that," she said. "Bob is perfectly clean and in his stall eating hay. It's about something else." A mischievous look crept across her face. "Rosie just arrived with her art kit to paint the clinic, and I had a brilliant idea . . ."

An hour later, Zoe led Raven out of his stall, fully tacked up. She was dressed in her best riding clothes, including a gold stock pin borrowed from her mother.

"Okay, Raven," she whispered as she reached up to tuck his throatlatch into the keeper. "You look perfect, and so do I. So let's go do this!"

As she led him across the yard, she noticed Mia crouched near the tack room fiddling with her boots. "Hi," Zoe said, smiling impishly as she remembered Becky's plan. "Where's Firefly? Shouldn't you be tacking him up? We'll be starting soon."

"If you must know, I was just on my way to get him." Mia straightened up and tossed her hair over her shoulder. "I saddled him early so I could have a cup of tea with Poppy before the clinic starts, but she was busy helping Susie fix her bridle and didn't have time."

"Oh." Zoe shrugged, gently pushing Raven's nose away so he wouldn't drool on her clean jacket. "Too bad."

"Yeah." Mia scowled, then sighed. "But whatever. This whole clinic thing hasn't turned out like I was imagining at all."

"What do you mean?" Zoe asked cautiously.

"Daddy was so excited about Poppy's visit," Mia said softly, staring into space almost as if she'd forgotten Zoe was there. "He actually canceled a business trip to be here. I thought it would be fun, just the three of us."

Suddenly, Zoe got it. Mia's father had always bought her anything she wanted—horses, saddles, clothes. But he wasn't always so willing to spend time with her. Zoe couldn't imagine how that felt. Even though her own father was far away in Los Angeles, she talked to him regularly—and she knew that if she ever really needed him, he would be there, no questions asked. She wasn't sure Mia could say the same about her dad, even though they lived in the same house.

That's the real reason Mia's been trying to keep Poppy all to herself, she realized. *It didn't have anything to do with me, or Susie, or the clinic—or even with Poppy.*

Mia took a deep breath, suddenly seeming to remember to whom she was talking. "Anyway, it's no big deal," she said with a sniff. "But, you know, sorry about the saddle pad or whatever. You didn't deserve that."

"No problem," Zoe said, glancing back at the yellow pad peeking out from beneath Raven's saddle. "I washed it last night, and it's good as new."

"Good." Mia flashed her a brief smile. "Anyway, I'd better get Firefly bridled. And when I see Jade I suppose I owe her an apology as well."

A moment later, Becky appeared with Bob. Zoe gulped, once again remembering Becky's plan. "Um, Mia, wait . . . ," she called, suddenly feeling a twinge of guilt over what they'd done.

Mia glanced back at her. "Look, you already won a spot in the clinic, Zoe," she said, sounding more like her usual imperious self. "You don't have to try to make yourself look better by making me late."

She hurried into Firefly's stall. Zoe steeled herself. A second later, a loud shriek rang through the yard. Mia burst out of the stall, pulling her startled horse along with her.

"All right, who did it?" she cried. "This isn't funny!"

The gray horse moved to the side, giving the entire yard a clear view of his hindquarters—including the big bright-blue smiley face painted on his rump.

Susie looked over from adjusting Darcy's bridle and giggled. "Looks like Firefly is in a happier mood than you are, Mia."

"Yeah, and now he matches Major and Darcy," Jade added, strolling over with Major.

Mia rounded on her, her eyes flashing fury. "You!" she shouted. "I knew you had to be behind this. Just petty revenge for that little accident yesterday, right? Very mature!"

As Jade's eyes widened, Zoe stepped forward, tugging Raven along behind her. "Don't yell at Jade, Mia," she said. "It's not her fault."

"It was my idea, actually," Becky said. "We thought this might remind you that riding is supposed to be fun."

Jade nodded. "And that we should all be working together to get better," she added. "Not competing against one another."

Mia glared at her. But before she could say anything, there was a clamor of voices from the yard entrance. Zoe turned and saw several Holloway riders striding in, leading their sleek, well-groomed horses.

"Well, hello, all," one of them, Alex, said with his usual smirk. "Glad to see you lot actually looking presentable for once."

His teammate, Callum, did a double take as he spotted Firefly's smiley face. "Well, *most* of you," he said. "Didn't anyone tell you this clinic is with Olympic-level riders? You might want to take it a bit more seriously than one of your little local pony camps."

Zoe tightened her grip on Raven's reins. Somehow, she and her friends had forgotten that Holloway would be here today. It was one thing to poke fun at Mia in front of her fellow Bright Fielders. But this . . .

All the Holloway riders were smirking by now. Mia glanced at Firefly, then tipped up her chin.

"For your information, it was one of the Olympic riders who inspired this," she informed the Holloway riders in her snootiest voice. "Poppy Addison has been giving us some exclusive riding instruction these past few days, and she's a strong believer that riding is supposed to be fun. So you might want to take that under advisement, hmm?"

With that, she clucked to Firefly and led him off without another word, leaving the Holloway riders exchanging confused looks. "Go, Mia!" Becky breathed, sounding awed.

"Yeah." Zoe turned away to hide her smile. "Now come on," she whispered to her friends. "Let's get out there. The clinic's about to start."

The clinic was long and exhausting and amazing. By the end, Zoe's head was spinning. There was so much more to learn, both for her and for Raven. She couldn't wait to practice all the new skills the Olympians had taught them!

But as tired as they were, they weren't too tired to take Poppy and her teammates for a thank-you ride on the beach that evening. As Zoe and Raven led the way at a gallop over the sand, having fun with all their friends, she couldn't stop smiling. Yes, there was still a lot to learn. But she and Raven had done really well today. Not only had they risen to their new challenge, but they had also both had so much fun. Now more than ever, Zoe knew they were ready for whatever came next!

The End

free REIN

The Steeplechase Secret

Turn the page to read a snippet of:

Free Rein: The Steeplechase Secret.

freeREIN
The Steeplechase Secret

NETFLIX
A NETFLIX
ORIGINAL SERIES

by
Jeanette Lane

SCHOLASTIC

1

An Island Visitor

Zoe breathed in the salty sea air and felt the breeze against her face. On impulse, she tugged off her boots and socks and dug her toes into the sand. She faced the ocean, curly wisps of hair fluttering in the wind. She closed her hazel eyes to feel the sun on her face, and—*BAM*!

"Raven!" Zoe yelped, stumbling forward. "Way to ruin the moment!" Raven, who had just playfully head-butted Zoe during her almost-perfect Zen moment, tossed his head in the air with a neigh. Zoe laughed and reached her arm around the beautiful black horse's neck. She took a deep breath and realized that *this* was the moment she had been working for—fighting for—ever since she had arrived on this small English island a couple of months earlier. Zoe leaned into Raven, giving him a hug. Raven snorted and dropped his coal-black head to rest on Zoe's shoulder.

"Hey, boy," she whispered into his tangled mane. "Isn't it great? No training. No Junior Nationals. No obligation to former owners who want you to win every competition." Zoe was referring to Raven's previous owner. Raven had been through a lot in his life: stolen as a foal and then shipwrecked, washing up on an island— the very island that was now their home. After that, he'd been horse-napped! But now he belonged to Zoe, and she belonged to him. It was the one thing of which Zoe was certain.

Maybe Raven hadn't minded the pressure of all the competitions, but Zoe was thrilled that life was back to normal—well, the new normal. Her old normal life was thousands of miles away, across a continent and an ocean, in Los Angeles, California. That's where she had lived her whole life until her mom decided to bring Zoe and her little sister, Rosie, to the island to visit their grandfather.

Zoe's mom had grown up on the island. She was used to being separated from the rest of the world, in a big, old stone house with a gorgeous garden and yard, where the only social life was at the local riding stables, Bright Fields. But surprisingly, Zoe was getting used to it, too.

Now her world revolved around Raven and Bright Fields. She'd made *horse-some* friends in Jade and Becky—together, they were Pony Squad! She'd also made a formidable frenemy in Mia, and she'd even had a couple of attempts at a proper boyfriend. First with Marcus, and then there was Pin. If things kept going well when Pin came back from Vienna, maybe they'd actually be able to make it "official" between them once and for all. Man, a lot had happened in a few months!

Zoe could hardly believe that her mom and Rosie had remained on the island just so Zoe could stay with Raven. "You really turned our world upside down, didn't you?" she said to him. As she thought about her old life, she gazed out at the ocean. A long, flat ferryboat caught her eye. Zoe hadn't seen any ferries dock at this side of the island. The ferries to the mainland usually came in at the pier, where there was an ice cream parlor and a couple of other attractions.

Zoe clucked to Raven and led him to the other side of the beach. "Let's get a better look," she said. Why would the boat be docking there? A little part of her told her she should just leave it alone. After all the drama with Raven and the horse stealers, she had promised her mom—and her dad, via Skype—that she would lie low and focus on her own responsibilities, like schoolwork—and Raven, of course. Still, Zoe could not contain her curiosity. On closer inspection, she could see a large SUV, a two-horse trailer, a bunch of building supplies like lumber and bags of sand, and many bales of hay and bags of grain.

"Looks pretty tasty, right?" Zoe said, patting Raven's neck, but she kept her eyes on the boat.

Just then, a boy walked to the bow and leaned over the railing. He wore a V-neck sweater with a crisp collared shirt and looked a couple of years older than Zoe. Soon, a man in a suit came up behind the boy and put a hand on his shoulder. Zoe wondered where they were headed. The island had several stables. What were the chances that they were bound for Bright Fields?

"We really should be getting back," Zoe said, as much to herself as to Raven. "Let's go, boy." But as she turned to go, Raven stayed put, still eyeing the ferry. He snorted.

"I know," Zoe said. "Something feels weird about it to me, too, but I'm sure it's nothing." Zoe looked at her horse, who did not seem convinced. "Not everything is a conspiracy!" she insisted, sounding a lot like her mom. Raven sighed and dropped his head. When Zoe lightly jangled the reins and rubbed his ear, he followed. She trudged back to where she'd discarded her footwear. "Ugh! Sand in the socks is not a good feeling with boots on," she mumbled to herself. Raven whinnied as if to laugh at her. "I know, I know. Serves me right."

By the time Zoe made it back to Bright Fields, the excess sand was bugging her so much that she let her feet dangle out of the stirrups.

"If you would stay *on* the horse, where you belong, these things wouldn't happen to you, Zoe," Mia declared. "You keep forgetting that Raven and you are horse and rider. It's not like you're mates."

Zoe scowled. "Speak for yourself. You and Firefly may have that relationship, but Raven and I have a special bond," Zoe said, patting Raven's neck.

Still in the saddle, she pulled off her boot and turned it over. Just as the sand started to spill out, Raven snorted and blew a cloud of sand grains right in Mia's face. Zoe tried (only a little) to contain her laughter, and Mia stomped off.

Zoe had come to learn that Mia could be a little less insufferable when she wanted to be—nice, even— *sometimes*. She'd still probably never stop making snarky comments or acting like she always knew best. But Mia had her reasons for being, well, Mia, and Zoe just had to keep reminding herself of that.

Jade and Becky were a far more welcome sight on Zoe's return to the stables. Pony Squad sat together in the tack room as Zoe cleaned the sand off her feet. "I got to see a super-sized ferry arrive and dock all the way over by the cove," she said to her friends. "That's kind of weird, right?"

Becky's expression grew serious. She tugged on her super-tight French braid, deep in thought. "Very weird," she agreed, always willing to consider the most unlikely explanations first. Becky was, after all, a firm believer in the so-called ghost pony who haunted the island. "Maybe it's a pirate boat! Or a boat full of *ghost* pirates! Or a gravy boat! Wait, that's not right . . ."

Jade, as usual, opted for a rational explanation instead. "Maybe the other pier was too crowded? It does get quite busy at this time of year." Just then, Mia waltzed into the tack room with Susie, her second in command, at her flank. In her hand Mia held a fancy cream-colored envelope embossed with a gold horseshoe.

"That ferry was just the first of many," she announced. She waved the envelope like an ornate fan. Zoe would never understand how Mia's poker-straight hair always looked salon fresh after hours at the stables. "A partnership from the mainland is investing in the old Grindlerock Racing Grounds. They're going to rehabilitate it and then sponsor a formal steeplechase event at the end of the month."

This news inspired the gasps of awe that Mia had hoped for—from everyone except Zoe.

"They're using that dock because it's better for oversized deliveries, like building equipment, trailers, and *top-ranked* European racehorses," Mia went on. She watched Zoe closely for her reaction, but Zoe didn't blink or even raise her eyebrows. "Isn't it thrilling?" Mia prompted.

"Oh, yes," Susie said on command. "Thrilling."

When Mia stared her down, Zoe finally commented. "Well, I might be thrilled, but you lost me at Grindlehock, and then you lost me again at steeplechase."

"It's *Grindlerock*," Mia corrected, "and it was once a stately racecourse that attracted tourists from the mainland every weekend of the competitive season. Of course, that was long before our time, but everyone knows it was lush and lovely."

"This is an island," Zoe stated. "We've ridden all over the place. How is there a big, fancy racetrack here that I've never seen?"

"Well," Mia replied, "Ireland and Australia are islands, too. Have you explored every square kilometer of those islands as well?"

"O-kay," Zoe replied. Mia had a point. The island did have all kinds of nooks and crannies that Zoe hadn't explored. This place was full of surprises! "But what are you so excited about, Mia? It's just a racetrack. You were a show jumper last I knew."

"Oh, Zoe," Mia said. "You are so provincially American. Steeplechase is not your stateside version of racing. It's not like the Triple Crown or other straight gallop-to-the-finish races. Steeplechase is a race with jumps. It is a quintessentially British event."

"Because they wear hats?" Zoe asked hopefully. Was there anything more British than the elegant spectator hats that they wore to weddings and parades and other posh affairs?

"Yes, because they wear hats," Mia confirmed. "And there will be hats at the Grindlerock opening event as well. You will all need one since you'll want to come cheer for Firefly and me."

"Hats? I'll make you a hat," Becky offered. "I have a bunch of old lampshades that I've been saving for a major crafting event—I knew they'd come in handy!"

"Um, no, thanks," Mia promptly replied.

"Wait. You're racing?" Jade asked Mia. "That sounds intense."

"Well, my dad met Mr. Cooke, the event promoter, on the mainland. They hit it off, of course. When Daddy told him about my performance at Junior Nationals, Mr. Cooke asked me to compete. This is the invitation." Mia paused and raised her eyebrows for effect. "I figure we need something to focus on now that Junior Nationals are over. Who's with me?" Mia immediately turned to Zoe.

"Um, no," Zoe answered. "Raven and I need some downtime. And training for a high-profile tourist attraction with hurdles and fancy hats is anything but that."

She and Raven needed a rest. Still, it was kind of exciting, knowing that the island would host a big event in just a few weeks.

"Why don't we ride out to this old track tomorrow and see it for ourselves?" Zoe tossed her chaps into her tack trunk. "The weather's supposed to be nice, and since we don't have to train, we could take a picnic and be gone all afternoon."

"Oh! I could bake something horse-some, like carrot-cake doughnuts," Becky suggested. "They're Bob's favorite. And mine." Bob was Becky's pony.

"That sounds delicious—and fun," Jade agreed.

"I know Raven could use more time exploring and less time in the ring practicing," Zoe said, loving her plan even more. "I could, too."

"An old racing track?" Becky said absentmindedly, not seeming to have heard a word Zoe just said. "Think of all the expectations and hope over the years. The adrenaline.

The rivalries. The heartbreak." She went on with a far-away look in her eyes. "I'll bet there are at least three ghost ponies trapped in the race grounds. Or maybe ghost *jockeys*," Becky whispered. Jade and Zoe turned to her. "Oh, did I say that out loud?" Becky asked, biting her lower lip.

"You did," Jade responded, giving her best friend a knowing smile. "But we'll pretend you didn't." Becky had a habit of letting her imagination get away with her. Jade preferred to stick to the facts. "We're not going on a whole ghost pony quest tomorrow. It's just a jaunt. For fun," Jade insisted. "To celebrate not having to train for Junior Nationals anymore."

Becky gave an enthusiastic smile, her braid bobbing with each nod. "Absolutely," she said. But something told Zoe that ghost ponies—or other kinds of ghosts—were still running wild in Becky's mind.

This will just be an innocent little field trip, Zoe told herself. *There won't be anything strange or mysterious at all. Right?*